LOVE JOY

AND SILLINESS

JAMAL MECKLAI

notionpress.com

INDIA • SINGAPORE • MALAYSIA

For my very own Guadalupe

ISBN 979-8-89929-310-8

In addition to the billions of people (most of them strangers) who have shown me so much kindness, I would like to specially thank

PRAVINA and KAVITA for their delighted and giggling editing and proofing;

AMELIA and NAYANA for their belief and enjoyment; and

OMENDU for his silliness and excellent design.

Love Joy and Silliness

The Pig Queen of The Tango

Early one Sunday morning, Shri Vindaloo lazed in bed running the inside of his paw against his cheek. He gazed at the sunshine dancing all over the room.

I wonder what it would be like to have a moustache, he thought, as a little bird twittered in his head.

He bounced out of bed and waddled over to the bathroom to the mirror and admired his slightly-hirsute jowls. "Hmmm...I think I'd have a lovely moustache," he said, and immediately set to shaving carefully.

He was interrupted twice – once by the call of nature and once by the call of the sea, when he stepped out to the verandah just a little more than half-shaved. Shri Vindaloo listened to the silences between the bird calls, which sounded to him like the Habanera from Carmen. As he swayed to the music his robe fell open, exposing his personal pig parts, and as the music crescendoed, he covered up with an explosive shrug and returned to the mirror.

"L'amour, l'amour," sang the pig patriarch lustily.

The razor swished and sailed and THERE!

Shri Vindaloo, complete with moustache, straw hat and a very cool pair of shades stepped out to the breakfast room.

A pretty little pig maiden was laying his breakfast on the table. "Good morning, Shri Vindaloo," she said.

"Isn't it a glorious day, Ramona?" said the patriarch smiling all across his beaming face.

"Oh! Look at you!" she said, clapping her paws together as she skipped over to him. "You have a moustache! It's so … so handsome!"

"Now, now, dear," said Shri Vindaloo, pleased inside himself. He tweaked her fat little jaw. "It is rather nice, isn't it?"

"Ooh!" she squealed. Delicate little grunts covered her body and she trotted from the room.

Smiling even more broadly than his face now, Shri Vindaloo sat at the table, and, tucking his napkin under his extensive chin, sniffed his Sunday breakfast – coconut husk scones, specially made for him by Gaspar Pig, overripe bananas and, of course, his special blend of feni-infused tea.

He let out an amiable burp and stretched his short legs. Mmmmm! Sunday, he thought lazily. Hmmm!

Ramona came in to clear the dishes. She was giggling a little. "Shri Vindaloo," she started shyly, "my mama's in town and…"

"Lola Flores!" The pig patriarch started from his chair, blinking his eyes. His new moustache quivered with enthusiasm. "When did she get into town?"

He smiled at Ramona but his thoughts were far away – in Andalusia, where he and Lola Flores had celebrated love for an exhausting and unforgettable week.

"She arrived yesterday. And she leaves for the Continent today."

"Oh, that Lola Flores," said Shri Vindaloo, knowingly.

He gathered his cane and twirled his moustache. "I must be off. I must see your mama." He planted a delicious little air kiss on her forehead and did a funny little tap-shuffle, his hooves clattering expertly on the earth floor. "Lola Flores! The Pig Queen of the Tango!" he said dramatically, and, with an Argentine flourish he was out on the street.

Ramona tittered about the breakfast dishes, swaying to the strains of her own tango. With a dreamy smile on her snout, she adjusted the flower behind her ear and remembered what her Mama often told her. "In time, my dear, in time."

Out on the street, Shri Vindaloo walked briskly towards the sea, acknowledging the boys, who were playing a smashing game of soccer with a still-full coconut. The coconut rolled towards Shri Vindaloo, who, inspired by everyday life, swung his significant form into a mighty pirouette and kicked the still-rolling coconut with his front right. It was a fine shot, careening for long seconds in the air before landing with a loud clatter against the tin shed which had been marked by the youngsters as the goal.

He tipped his hat amid squeals of "Shri Vindaloo, come and join us."

"Sorry lads. I have to go dance with my past and with my future," and with his slightly foolish grin, he hailed a passing pedicab limousine.

Young Francis, whose father Shri Vindaloo had helped when he had lost a bundle in the toddy business, stopped his vehicle and peered out. "Good Sunday, Shri Vindaloo. It's a fine day. That's a fine moustache you're sporting, sir."

Shri Vindaloo beamed at him, quite pleased. "Do you know the Tango Club, Francis?"

"It's a bit early for that, isn't it, sir?"

"It's never too early to dance," said the pig patriarch, as he pursed his lips into a little heart-shaped "O" and settled in to listen to the now-soulful silences between the calls of the seagulls.

The pedicab limousine ambled through the still sleepy town. In the back, Shri Vindaloo, excited by the prospects of seeing Lola Flores again, began to sing in loud fervent grunts. He didn't know all the words to the song he was singing and it sounded all rather modern to young Francis, who, inspired by having the pig patriarch in his cab, started driving faster and faster and faster and faster.

Shri Vindaloo rattled and rolled against the cushions in the back, and began to draw deeper breaths till his notes came fewer and farther between. "Stop!" he grunted as loudly as he could, for they had almost sped by the Tango

Club, which looked like it was just stirring from Saturday night, yawning, stretching a bit, reaching for the feni and orange juice.

"Oh, sorry, Shri Vindaloo," said Francis, pulling up sharply. The pig patriarch reached into his breast pocket to pay the fare, but Francis disarmed him away.

With a funny little skip, Shri Vindaloo thanked the young pig and disappeared under the silent neon sign. The music was still playing, of course, and there was a tired couple still on the floor. He was a famous, retired soccer player, who had once scored two goals in the World Cup but was sent off the field for kissing the referee too much. His wife, who always wore a black straw hat – they said she even kept it on in bed – was reclining in his arms as the rhythm slowed.

Shri Vindaloo blinked slightly, his eyes getting used to the delicious smoke. There was a little breeze blowing beside him. He turned his large head slowly.

And there she was. Lola Flores! Like some pig version of paradise, she was smiling and laughing and smoking a cigarette in a long holder all at the same time.

"Shall we dance?" said the pig patriarch gallantly.

The orchestra struck up Kiss of Fire and they glided onto the floor, swaying and trotting in such a tumultuous way that even the cadaverous waiters stopped doing nothing and watched.

"I'm glad you came this morning, liebling," for that's what she always called him. "I leave for Paris in an hour."

"Ah! Lola Flores!" said Shri Vindaloo as she threw her head back, her lissom neck rippling before his face.

They swayed there together for long minutes, looking like a pair of plump birds of paradise.

"Soon, liebling, soon," she whispered to him in her throaty voice, when the music stopped. "Soon we will dance across Europe again."

"Ah! Lola Flores!" said Shri Vindaloo.

"It won't be long now," she said, once again the twinkling pig star of international stage and screen. She brushed her pretty snout across his moustache and, calling for her retinue of bags and bouquets, swept out of the club.

Shri Vindaloo sat at the empty chair by the dance floor smiling dreamily. He played with his moustache and sipped the champagne a waiter had thoughtfully set near him.

Suddenly, he got up and strode to the dressing room. "Antonio!" he called out, settling into the plush red velvet upholstered barber chair that he himself had installed at the Tango Club a few years before. "Could you please shave off my moustache?"

Swedish Massage

It was a Wednesday. He could tell because he was awakened by the *malishwali*. She always came to see him on Wednesdays. Except that time when she was having a daughter, which was a day just like this one, except that he had been awakened by the telephone instead, several hours later.

The *malishwali* flipped him over expertly with her paws, as usual partly shy and partly professional. He rolled his ample form sinuously and his left leg kicked a few times in an incandescent early morning rhythm. "Hkhaaao!" he called out. Madame Olga trotted tentatively backwards, looking away as the sheets went flying.

Shri Vindaloo was awake.

"Madame Olga," he squealed, "like the sun you are always here on Wednesdays." And he shuffled his naked pig form to the bathroom. Madame Olga, modest despite her profession, looked away as a hint of crimson tinted her sturdy pinkness.

A tralala mixed with a heavy torrent later, Shri Vindaloo, elegant beyond words in a resplendent Japanese day-robe, entered with a flourish. Madame Olga, in her efficient Swedish way, had already changed into her one-shoulder leopardskin massage outfit and had converted the daybed into a massage table, with a leopard print cover, of course.

"Isn't it a wonderful day, Madame Olga," Shri Vindaloo said grandly.

"Yes, Shri Vindaloo," she said proudly, "and might I say you look like you need a good rubdown."

"Oh, yes, Madame Olga. The life of a patriarch has its demands."

She cluck-grunted as only she could. "OK. All right. Pay attention. Down you go now," she said imperiously and even an impartial observer could see her neck glands deepen from their already shy fuschia shade.

In a few moments the silence between the sounds of the birds twittering and the sea surfing was suffused with the soft sigh-grunts of Shri Vindaloo in delight. Madame Olga was an expert and her paws were strong yet gentle as a late summer rain. And how they caressed his flesh! Shri Vindaloo found himself dreaming lavender thoughts, new juices rushed from nowhere up to his undulating porkskin. My weekly vitamins, he thought; I must remember to get Madame Olga a real leopardskin massage table.

For clearly, Madame Olga, in her private modest way, loved leopardskin.

It reminded her of her younger days when, with Pig Bull, the ugly and dashing big game hunter, she had left her family's humble sty in the far north of Sweden to go to Senegal in search of leopards. Pig Bull had been eaten alive before her very eyes on a safari and she had fainted. She remained in a coma for days, they said, and developed a palliative case of amnesia when she recovered.

It was only years later, after she had moved to Goa and established herself as the premier practitioner of Swedish massage in the little villages around Panaji that she had been able to trace her fondness for leopardskin, her past and the paternity of her sometimes frighteningly self-willed daughter.

Monella, her daughter, was difficult as a child, to say the least, and as she grew beyond pig maidenhood, became progressively more so – she had dreams of going to Hollywood.

As Madame Olga worked, Shri Vindaloo's delighted sighs became louder and louder and grunter and faster.

Suddenly, the door flew open and Monella burst in, wearing a translucent slip-type dress which showed off her considerable charms – she was beautiful and sexy and almost frightening. And, with a thank-you air-kiss at her mother, she leapt with a feverish grunting onto the patriarch's broad pulsating back and began to stomp and pummel his rich flesh. His cries got shriller, now resembling the squawking of the crows outside, and, as she dug her long brightly-coloured nails into his ample meat, Shri Vindaloo melted to the sheets.

"Ah, Monella!" sighed the patriarch.

"Oh, Monella," bemoaned Madame Olga. "Why must you always do that?"

"It's like you always told me Mama," said Monella, inspecting her fingernails, "a mother's work is never done. I'm just helping you finish off."

She jumped nimbly off Shri Vindaloo's now completely relaxed frame. "Now, mother dear, I have something to discuss with Shri Vindaloo, so..."

Madame Olga cast a fond and despairing look at Shri Vindaloo who had rolled his enormous form over and was gingerly stretching all his pink limbs at them, still grunting sweetly.

She knew her daughter's wiles and she knew Shri Vindaloo's weaknesses and she knew ... but, it happened so often and Shri Vindaloo didn't seem to mind. So, she smiled at the vulnerable patriarch and discreetly left the room.

****

And it was a Wednesday, years later, that Shri Vindaloo, enjoying the monsoon spray on the verandah of the Pig Enterprises building, received a giant bouquet of lavender carnations flown over by special jet from Hollywood, California.

He grunted, did a silly little jig dance around the jetlagged messenger pig and tipped him with a box of cigars.

Love in Leningrad

"Be undressed and waiting, my precious angel!"

Shri Vindaloo had picked up an envelope with a brilliant stamp that was waiting by his breakfast tray one morning; it was postmarked KHAB ROV K, which excited him so much that he tore the envelope open and, slipping out the also-torn sheet of letter paper, those were the first words he read.

Dressed in just a loose robe, he was, in a sense, already undressed, and, of course, he was waiting. He had, over the years, received many love notes, suggestive and otherwise, but "…my precious angel" was more than any love-call he could have even dreamed of. He immediately threw off his robe, and, completely naked in the breakfast room, carefully unfolded the letter.

It was from Galina, a brilliant and very fetching pig he had met at a dinner in Khabarovsk, when he had been in the Soviet Union nearly a year earlier. They had spent much of the evening with a large group of people feasting on cabbage and potatoes and cauliflower – the only three things that were available in the market, which their hostess had turned into eleven delicious courses. And there was vodka, of course. Almost more than was necessary.

Galina sat very close to him all evening and, keeping their glasses filled with vodka, they talked and talked and talked about life, about love, about the difficulties of living in the Soviet Union, but how she wouldn't leave even if she could. She was studying genetics and, truly a renaissance woman, would burst into poetry from time to time, much of which he didn't understand When he told her about himself and his delighted life, she leaned back, eyes flashing through her thick spectacles and blew pouty kisses at him. She had a delicious throaty laugh that sounded like a bouquet of wayward promises.

The party broke up around 4 in the morning but Galina had to go back to the small flat she shared with her family; Shri Vindaloo walked back to the hotel with a few others who had been at the dinner. The post-mortem was about all the interesting people they had met – turned out Galina was a major star at the university in Leningrad and was in Khabarovsk for the holidays visiting her parents.

Shri Vindaloo had taken her address in Leningrad and, on his return to Goa, had sent her a coconut, painted in his own naif style with lips puckered in a crimson kiss – he thought it looked like him.

That was a few months ago. And here she was – be undressed and waiting, my precious angel.

He raced through the rest of the letter where she said how much she had loved meeting him and how much she adored the coconut – she kissed the coconut lips every night and kept it by her bed till it started to smell. She would be in Leningrad in October, but it may be too cold and if he could come there in September, she'd find a way to see him.

It was late August and the monsoon in Goa was practising its exit with occasional thunderstorms and magical rain. Shri Vindaloo scratched his coconut-head and called out to Eunice Pig, his lady pig for all seasons, and, as he heard her at the door, hurriedly pulled his robe back on.

Eunice Pig was from the same village as he and had been a celebrated fado singer in her youth. As a young pig, Master Vindaloo spent several evenings lying on his back outside her house listening to her practice for her concerts. Her illustrious career, unfortunately, ended suddenly when her husband, Santan, had made a terrible drunken scene while she was singing at the Cardinal's house one Easter. It was so shameful that, for several months, Eunice Pig didn't leave the house even to go to Mass!

It was during this period that Shri Vindaloo, who loved her and her singing, sent her a special gift – a parrot that he tried to train to sing fado; in the note he said, "Teach him to sing like you."

This opened Eunice Pig's heart and she came to visit Shri Vindaloo a few mornings later, where she found him buried in papers and other business bits while in the midst of his usual morning repast. She immediately set to straightening the papers and, in time, other things, till she was indispensable to his extravagant life.

They loved each other at a seemly distance, even though Santan had long disappeared. He bought her a small place close to the Pig Enterprises building and, sometimes, on quiet evenings, before the tide picked up, he would hear her – and the parrot – practising fado duets.

She smiled as she came in, "Shri Vindaloo, you look amazedly excited."

"Read this, Eunice Pig," handing her the letter.

She read it quickly, blushing a bit, and said, "Oh, that's so… so wonderful Shri Vindaloo, you must go to Leningrad. I'll cancel all your appointments after the tenth of next month and ask the Chamber of Commerce to delay the award ceremony – I'll book you on a flight to Helsinki and then the overnight train to Leningrad." She stopped. "But you haven't even had your breakfast yet."

He settled down and she called for a fresh breakfast, which he nibbled at while she gave/took instructions on various business matters.

On the night of September 11th, Shri Vindaloo found himself in Helsinki, boarding the overnight train to Leningrad. He blessed Eunice Pig for the seven millionth time – what would I ever do without her, he thought. She had made all the inquiries and found out that the only way he could visit the Soviet Union alone – and not with a group, as he had the previous time – would be on a business visa. Fortunately, the BioPig division of Pig Enterprises was working on analysing the coconut genome so more people in the world could benefit from the joyous effects of coconuts and sunshine. And, as Eunice Pig's investigations discovered, the University of Leningrad was expert in studying the genetics of tropical plants. Shri Vindaloo smiled to himself; Galina was studying genetics at the university.

The Finnish pig girl who was his concierge on the train was, of course, charmed by Shri Vindaloo, who was singing, "Galina, Galina, Galina" as he approached the train, but she was worried about the large crate of coconuts that he carried. "But what will you tell Soviet customs," she asked him. "You can't tell them about Galina."

Shri Vindaloo, in his enthusiastically forthright way had told Eevi, for that was her name, all about Galina and even showed her the letter.

"I will give the customs man a coconut," said Shri Vindaloo, with a delighted smile.

"Let me call my friend Geevi," said Eevi. "He works in customs at the Finnish border, but, more importantly, he is from Georgia and is a great romantic. You can tell him your story."

And so, blowing Eevi a kiss, Shri Vindaloo boarded the train and was off.

A little over two hours later, the train pulled into the Finland/Soviet Union border in Estonia, and as Shri Vindaloo was trying to open the window to sniff the air, there was a peremptory knocking at the door of his coupe. He jumped up as the door was pushed open and a short, well-built man slipped in shutting the door behind him.

"Shri Vindaloo from Goa?" he said in a soft voice.

"Yes, yes, I am," in an excited squeak.

"I am Geevi, Eevi's friend. She has told me about you. I have been to Goa, many years ago, when I was allowed to travel – before all this." He gestured at the uniform and the epaulettes.

Shri Vindaloo melted, "Oh, I wish I had known. Where did you go? Did you like it?"

"Like it? I loved it. I rented a motorcycle and travelled all over – ah! the air, the beaches, the feni, the food and the Goan pig ladies – I would like to come back."

"Please, please come as my guest. Let me give you my address"

"Yes, of course. But first we must sort out your papers, we don't have too long. And I need to read that letter," Geevi smiled conspiratorially.

Shri Vindaloo pulled the letter from his breast pocket, and he retrieved his passport and other papers from his valise.

Geevi first studied the travel documents and signed on two or three pages, nodding. And, then sitting on the bunk, read Galina's letter, quietly but with an ever-expanding smile. "Shri Vindaloo, my friend, I wish you only love forever. Go to Galina, but be careful – it may be dangerous for her."

"But why?" said Shri Vindaloo. "Everybody loves a lover, they say."

"Not in the Soviet Union," said Geevi. "The Soviet Union has no sense of joy and frowns sternly upon love across the Iron Curtain – I know. That's why I was demoted to this," pointing again at his uniform. "You will be met at Leningrad station by a host from the university, who will be assigned to ensure that you do not stray from the agenda they will have set for you. Do NOT tell him anything about Galina. You must meet her by chance at the university – she must be planning something. Good luck."

There were two sharp blasts of the train whistle and Geevi got up to go. Shri Vindaloo embraced him, pushing his address on him and gave him a special coconut from the collection.

"Thank you," said Geevi. "Who knows, maybe the work you do with Galina will bring some sunshine to us all."

Shri Vindaloo was, as was often the case, happy and confused. He lay down and fell asleep.

He awoke after several hours, rubbing the cobwebs of jet lag from his eyes. The coupe attendant was before him with tea.

"Thank you, thank you," said Shri Vindaloo, taking the silver mug from him. Remembering, he reached into his trousers and found a loose currency note, which he handed over to the smiling pig. Passing him a coconut, he said, "Might you be able to open this for me?"

"Yes sir, yes sir, of course," quickly backing out of the coupe.

In no time at all, the attendant was back proudly bearing his coconut aloft on a silver platter; the coconut looked like it had had a bit of a battle, but there was a hole poked through the top – apparently with a screwdriver – and in the hole was a silver straw.

As Shri Vindaloo slurped with delight, the attendant said, apologetically, "If you wish, sir, we have only caviar and champagne."

"Yes please," delightedly, and more currency notes changed hands.

The ride into Leningrad was a tasteful blur and as the train pulled in, Shri Vindaloo was mid-way through the second bottle of champagne. An excellent repast, he thought, as he struggled to rouse himself from the cushions to greet his new life.

There was, again, the peremptory knock on the coupe door which opened to reveal a stern-looking officer, who said, "Shuree Venadaloo? From Goa? To meet the University of Leningrad?"

"Yes, yes, thank you," said Shri Vindaloo, smiling. "And its Shri not Shuree, and Vindaloo not Venadaloo. But it doesn't matter. I'm sure I would sound funny speaking Russian."

The man was not amused and asked the attendant to get Shri Vindaloo's bags off the train. He said, "I am Andrei Korovski and I will be your liaison for your stay in Leningrad. Did you have a comfortable journey?"

"Yes, yes," began Shri Vindaloo, "there was cham.."

But he was cut off as Andrei had stepped off the train and was reaching back to assist Shri Vindaloo. "We must go to immigration and customs. This way."

The immigration officer was a burly lady who smiled when she saw his passport, "Ah, from India. A friend. You know Raj Kapoor?"

"I have met him, yes," said Shri Vindaloo remembering when Raj Kapoor flew down to Goa to ask him to be a dance consultant for "Bobby", which unfortunately Shri Vindaloo had to turn down. "A very handsome man," he said to the lady officer.

"And what brings you to Leningrad?"

He blurted, "To see Ga.."

Andrei interrupted smoothly, "He has meetings at the University of Leningrad," handing over the appointment documents.

"And you will be staying...where?" this to Andrei.

"The Palace Bridge Hotel."

"Ah, thank you. Goodbye, Mr. Friend of Raj Kapoor. Enjoy your visit."

Shri Vindaloo smiled at her and it was all he could do to resist giving her a coconut, but he was beginning to understand that he must not be "natural" here.

Andrei was already moving him towards the exit.

Shri Vindaloo looked excitedly about the terminal, thinking that maybe Galina had come to the airport to receive him. Was that her? Or that? He realized that he didn't remember very clearly what she looked like, but he caught a flash of light – could that be her? She had a gold tooth that glinted when it caught the light, and he thought he heard her distinctive laugh.

By then they were at the car and, delight of delights, there was a female driver – he remembered that in the Soviet Union women often had jobs that were generally taken by men. Quite modern, he thought, as he smiled and half-bowed to the lady driver.

Andrei, returned from putting the luggage into the trunk, and snapped something in Russian at the driver, who started the car. Shri Vindaloo tried to smile at her in the rear-view mirror – she was, indeed, quite attractive – but she kept her eyes on the road.

Andre was explaining how things would run. It sounded militaristic – tomorrow morning: breakfast at 8:30; meeting at the university with the President of the Genetics department: at 9:30;...

Shri Vindaloo interrupted. "No, no, my friend. I can't meet anybody, let alone the President, till at least 11 in the morning – I need to wake up slowly, as I do in Goa. After all, who knows what time we'll go to bed tonight."

"Ah, Shuree Vendaloo," said Andrei almost agreeably. "I will be with you from now till the time you go to sleep. I will come up to your room after we finish dinner and whatever else you would like to do and wait till you are abed before I leave."

"Does the hotel have a restaurant, with a floor show?"

"Floor show?" Andrei seemed confused. "There is a restaurant with a band," looking at his watch. "But the music only starts at 9 and it's not yet 8 o'clock now."

"Oh, that's great," said Shri Vindaloo quite excited now. "I'll need to shower and change and we can have some vodka, no?"

"Yes, but tomorrow's meeting..."

"Yes, but we must have vodka tonight," said Shri Vindaloo, closing the conversation and looking out the window. He thought he caught a smile on the driver's face.

"That's the Neva river," said Andrei in a small voice. "And here we are at the hotel."

The hotel looked quite grand but terribly run down. A surly doorman stood at the entrance and made no attempt to welcome him. Andrei was out of the car and getting the bags. And, yes, that was a smile on the driver's face.

They swept-stumbled into the lobby; Andrei, with Shri Vindaloo's arm in a rather firm grip, marched over to the desk and muttered something in Russian. Shri Vindaloo recognized a few words, like 'university' and 'India' and 'president'. Amazingly the formalities took no time at all and they were in a lift going up to the 13th floor; Andrei carried the bags.

The lift was old and smelled as if someone had just farted in there. Shri Vindaloo twitched his nose; Andrei stood stock still. When the lift doors finally opened he saw a semi-shabby corridor with a bull-necked pig lady at a desk which separated the lift lobby from the rooms.

"Dezhurnaya," muttered Andrei under his breath, handing her the entry slip.

"Ah, the keeper of the keys," said Shri Vindaloo, smiling at her. He remembered from his previous visit that this creature was King Queen and Knave of the particular hotel floor and, as Shri Vindaloo already had plans to bring Galina up to his room, he needed to be on her right side. And he also had to find a way to get rid of Andrei.

She rudely pushed the key across the table to Andrei and half-smiled at Shri Vindaloo, who wrestled his arm out of Andrei's grasp.

"Un momento," he said, reaching into his carry-on bag and bringing out a coconut, which he proffered to the dezhurnaya.

She took it, happy but confused. She clearly didn't know what to do with it. Shri Vindaloo pantomimed taking a knife and chopping the top of the coconut off and then lifting it to his lips and "Ahhhh!"

"Ahhhh," she said, now fully smiling.

They turned for the corridor and Shri Vindaloo thought he heard a fart. He didn't turn back though – wouldn't do to embarrass an important friend.

Andrei was true to his word and, other than when Shri Vindaloo went to the bathroom, stuck closely to him as he unpacked his suitcases. He glanced curiously at the contents, snorting suddenly when Shri Vindaloo took out three pairs of dark glasses and arranged them by the bedside. When he got to the clothes, Andrei suddenly turned into a valet and neatly hung up the suits, the various brightly-coloured trousers and printed shirts, snorting softly to himself much of the time.

"And aha! Here we are," said Shri Vindaloo, as he pulled out a particularly grotesque-looking necktie, which he handed to Andrei. "For you, my friend Andrei."

Andrei was shocked (by the tie), terrified (that he may have to wear it) and truly distressed (that he may have showed some emotion).

"No, no, Shuree Veendoola, I can't accept that. I can't accept anything. Rules."

"There are no rules in research," said Shri Vindaloo with a flourish. "Come replace that ugly thing around your neck with this tie and let's go down and get some vodka."

Andrei was, for the first time in his career, suddenly nervous and his vice-like grip on Shri Vindaloo's arm seemed looser as they trotted down the corridor to the lift. There was a bit of an altercation at the dezhurnaya's table and Shri Vindaloo's friend was looking a little down in the mouth as a truly frightening matronly pig was holding the coconut and shouting at her. The farty smell appeared more intense.

"Good evening," said Shri Vindaloo sweetly and entered the lift with Andrei, now more limply attached to his arm.

The lift stopped on the second floor and the door opened into a dark, cavernous room that was decorated like a set from a 1940's Hollywood film. It was also, of course, seriously run down, the carpet fraying and much of the furniture covered with dust. There were a few customers scattered randomly around the room and the band – a guitar, bass and piano – were just setting up.

They found a table and Andrei, at his officious best, clicked his fingers for service. There were four waiters lazing by the bandstand; two of them looked up at Andrei's signal but continued their conversation. As Andrei fumed, clapping his hands once or twice, Shri Vindaloo took out a currency note and started cleaning his fingernails with it. A waiter suddenly appeared with a bottle of vodka and two glasses.

"Ice?" said Shri Vindaloo and drew another currency note from his pocket.

The waiter scurried away and returned after several long minutes. Shri Vindaloo did the honours, pouring rather large shots for both Andrei and himself. Andrei declined saying he was on duty.

"But there's no duty with me – I won't be able to work with the university if people have to follow rules and suffer duty."

Andrei relented, "But just one," he said.

They clinked glasses, Shri Vindaloo took a swallow, Andrei downed his glass. Shri Vindaloo topped him up.

And the music started. A saccharine standard from a few decades ago – Feelings. A large man across the room sang along dreadfully, swigging vodka directly from the bottle. As the song ended, he stood up – he was even bigger than he had looked and when he got up Shri Vindaloo saw that there was a very svelte woman on another chair at the table – and raising his arms crooned "Feelings" as one of his underlings took a reasonably fat wad of currency notes to the band.

Shri Vindaloo called out "Marina, Marina, Marina" and held out a pile of currency notes in his paw. To his delight, the guitarist smiled at him and the band started playing an instrumental version of the Italian classic. Very versatile, thought Shri Vindaloo, as he hummed along; it was all he could do to not shout out, Galina, Galina, Galina to the chorus.

Mid-song, a not too svelte and large bosomed woman in a short sequined dress appeared at his side. Andrei clicked his fingers signalling her to leave. But she had her eye on Shri Vindaloo's fine form and, of course, the stack of notes in his hand. She sidled closer. Andrei got more peremptory and tried to push her away. But the song ended and Shri Vindaloo turned to Andrei, "Can you take this money to the band, please."

Torn between "protecting" Shri Vindaloo and following his wishes, Andrei rushed over to the band stand looking back at the same time and almost fell over an outstretched chair. The lady meanwhile almost sat in Shri Vindaloo's lap, "I Valentina," she said as her unsound perfume almost intoxicated Shri Vindaloo. "You wish sex?"

But Andrei was back before Shri Vindaloo could do anything and he pulled her away. She started shouting at him and tried to scratch his face. But Andrei was quite strong and pushed her further away. She continued shouting, the band stopped playing and another large man, even more officious-looking than Andrei, showed up and whispered something to Andrei.

Andrei told Shri Vindaloo, "We have to go. He is from the police."

Blowing a kiss at Valentina, Shri Vindaloo got up and quite happily – he had to save himself for Galina and it had been a long day of travel – accompanied Andrei back to the lift.

At floor 13, they found a dour dezhurnaya at the desk; clearly Shri Vindaloo's friend had been moved. Andrei wordlessly got the room key and escorted Shri Vindaloo to his room. The bed had been very nicely turned down, Shri Vindaloo swiftly changed into his pyjamas and, with an extended yawn, lay down on the bed.

"Thank you very much Andrei. Can you arrange champagne and caviar for my breakfast at...hmmm...OK... 9 am please?"

And with that, Shri Vindaloo fell into a deep sleep.

He slept through a discreet knocking following by a loud pounding on his door and only awoke when Andrei shook his sleeping shoulder. "Shuree Vendaloo, wake up, it's already 9:30. I have been able to shift the president's meeting to 10:30 – I told him you were jet lagged. Please, get up. Your breakfast's here."

Shri Vindaloo rubbed his eyes and smiled awake. He had been, of course, dreaming of Galina, who in the dream was a dynamic combination of Valentina and the driver from the university with her distinctive laugh and shimmering gold tooth; they were rolling around on a bed of coconuts.

He noticed, slightly disappointed, that Andrei had ditched the loud tie he gave him in favour of the colourless scrap he wore when he met him at the airport. But he smiled when he saw the room service tray with champagne, caviar and a sliced-open coconut. He hurried to the toilet, abluted and returned to see that Andrei had drawn the curtains.

"What a glorious day," said Shri Vindaloo as he directed Andrei to mix a glass of champagne and coconut water for both of them. Andrei, of course, poured only one glass and, as Shri Vindaloo tucked in, told him, "There is a young researcher who will be joining the meeting with the president; she is an expert in genetic studies and has been brought in from the Soviet Far East for three days only. So we should hurry."

More than excited, Shri Vindaloo downed his breakfast cocktail and poured another which he carried to the shower. "Andrei, can you pick something from the cupboard for me to wear please?"

Freshly showered and wearing a constantly-widening smile, a naked Shri Vindaloo bounced out of the bathroom to greet a shocked and blushing Andrei who was, in any case, flummoxed by the sartorial choices available in Shri Vindaloo's wardrobe. With difficulty he settled on a smart shirt with multi-coloured stripes and a thankfully simple pair of slacks; the trauma was choosing between a super-trendy jacket with multi-coloured checks and a sweater with a lizard-print pattern.

Shri Vindaloo acknowledged Andrei's selection, picking the lizard-print sweater and pulled a bright pink scarf from his luggage – Eunice Pig had done a stellar job packing for his trip; he must remember to get her some chocolates and caviar when he returned. They left the room to the tune of yet another dezhurnaya, yet larger and sterner, and zipped down to the lobby.

Colour, like love and other joyous animals, was not a public function in the Soviet Union so as Shri Vindaloo, with his modest entourage of Andrei and a porter carrying the case of coconuts, strode through the lobby it was all eyes-on-him. It was also likely that word of the modest tangle with Valentina had got around – indeed, judging from the dezhurnaya switching, it seemed that Shri Vindaloo, contrary to everything he had been advised by Geevi, had made a substantial entrance into Leningrad.

He resolved to hide his incandescent light from here on and slunk into the waiting car. He was delighted to see the same lovely lady driver who had a supporting role in his dream, and, of course, his smile and sweetness returned. Andrei delivered instructions to the driver and turned to Shri Vindaloo. "Things have been going a bit too …mmm… loudly," he said quietly and tried to return the flamboyant necktie.

"No, no," said Shri Vindaloo determinedly. "That's for you and all your trouble."

"It has been no trouble, sir, I mean Shree Vendaloo."

They drove along the river. Shri Vindaloo put the window down a bit to taste the bracing autumn air and his pink scarf flapflapped all around him. Andrei was looking increasingly nervous; Shri Vindaloo patted his thigh to calm him down and they pulled into a very sombre institutional-looking building.

"Ah," said Andrei, "the University…"

Shri Vindaloo looked out the car window and, try as he might to be calm, he almost jumped out of his seat.

There, waiting, though fully dressed, in the entrance foyer of the university was – it had to be – Galina. He immediately remembered her exactly as she was. She was wearing a tight sweater – grey, of course – and dark slacks. And smiling just as he remembered.

Andrei got out of the car and turned to the trunk from where he was retrieving the coconuts. He said, "Shree Vendaloo, this is Comrade Mitsura who has been brought to Leningrad all the way from the Soviet Far East to discuss the research project with you. Comrade Mitsura, I am

Andrei Korovski, and this is Shree Vendaloo from Goa for the coconut project."

Shri Vindaloo jumped out of the car and started to reach out to her, but she twinkled a smile at him and very properly turned away from his outstretched arm. He stopped in surprise – this shouldn't be how you treat your precious angel, he thought.

"Later, Shri Vindaloo," she whispered. "We can't appear to know each other or…"

The driver girl was watching them greet each other.

"Shri Vindaloo, I am so excited to meet you," said Galina, now smiling openly at him. "I have been studying tropical genomes for a long time, but, here, in the cold Soviet Union, it is difficult to get a real touch and feel of tropicality."

"But I can't call you Miss Mitsura," said Shri Vindaloo, recovering some degree of poise. "I must have your intimate name."

"Galina, I am Galina for you, Shri Vindaloo. And what a curious sweater you are wearing," she said with a throaty laugh. "Did you know that lizards are the only creatures that have two male procreative organs.?"

"No," said Shri Vindaloo, amazed. "I did not know that, Galina, how interesting. But, how do they…" he trailed off.

Galina laughed that throaty laugh again. "I have no idea Shri Vindaloo. Maybe we can study lizards as well as coconuts."

The conversation brought them to the door of the university building. They were walking quite close together and Andrei coughed loudly as he tried to insert himself between the two of them, but he was hampered by the large sack of coconuts he was carrying.

Shri Vindaloo opened the door for Galina and, quite naturally, she brushed against him as she went in. "Thank you, Shri Vindaloo."

He was, of course, almost vibrating with excitement and trying to keep it from showing.

Galina turned to Andrei, "Comrade Korovski, I have been instructed to take Shri Vindaloo directly to the President on the seventh floor."

"But," began Andrei, "my instructions were to take Shree Vendaloo to the President's conference room ..."

"That's also on the seventh floor, Comrade Korovski."

They entered the lift, Andrei dragging the sack of coconuts behind him. When he looked up, Galina was looking at Shri Vindaloo, who was precariously close to her, and looking at her in a strange, familiar way."

"Seven please," she said.

Andrei put the sack down and pressed 7.

The lift lurched upwards and Shri Vindaloo half fell against Galina, who had to take his hand to help him off.

"Oh, dear," Shri Vindaloo apologized, "I am a bit groggy."

"Oh yes, you've just arrived." Galina took a semi-step back. "Did you have a good flight, Shri Vindaloo? And a good night?"

"Well, Andrei took good care of me, particularly in the night club. And I slept like a baby." He smiled, turning briefly to Andrei, who was looking at his feet. "But with decidedly non-baby-like dreams."

"How do you know what babies dream, Shri Vindaloo? You must tell me." Galina laughed.

"Here we are," said Andrei, trying to get his controlled demeanour back.

The lift doors opened to a strikingly attractive young pig, "Shri Vindaloo, welcome to the University of Leningrad. We are so proud that you have come to see us."

Shri Vindaloo smiled and shook the young pig's pretty paw.

"I am Masha," she said smiling, "the President's very special assistant."

And Shri Vindaloo noticed that she was very special indeed. Tall – statuesque actually – and dressed like a Western fashion model. The President was well looked after, he thought.

"Thank you," he said, retrieving his hand. "And this is Galina, who..."

"We know Comrade Mitsura," said Masha, still smiling. "The President had to leave suddenly. He has apologized and said that you – you and Galina – can use his private study to begin your discussings."

She looked around and caught Andrei's bleating face. "Ah, there you are Comrade Korovski, two hours late."

Strict and stern now. "You take those coconuts to the fifth floor laboratory and come back with the receipt."

She turned her back on poor Andrei and escorted Shri Vindaloo and Galina towards a velvet-lined door, which she caressed with her free hand.

She softened again, now that Andrei was gone. "Galya, make sure Shri Vindaloo is comfortable. I'll send some tea in shortly."

Hmmm, thought Shri Vindaloo, the President seems like an interesting pig and this beautiful Masha – she seems to know Galina quite well. He leaned forward and opened the door to the ante-chamber, and once again Galina – more slowly this time – brushed past him as she entered.

As the door closed, they were in each other's' arms, kissing each other, feeling their bodies with their bodies and, of course, grunting quite loudly.

Galina stopped and pushed him away a little bit. "We must be quieter, Shri Vindaloo."

And, again, she threw herself upon him with so much urgency that he almost fell backwards. She was kissing him feverishly and working the buttons on his clothes. And suddenly, Shri Vindaloo was naked, all his clothes in a pool on the floor by his feet.

She stepped back. "Let me look at you. You are so beautiful. And I see you are not a lizard."

Shri Vindaloo was, of course, almost beyond control. "Come to me, my precious angel." He pulled her to him and began to struggle with her fasteners.

"I need a minute, Shri Vindaloo, I have to arrange certain things," she said. Caressing his nakedness, she led him to the sofa and, with a soft kiss, she said, "Lie down there. I'll be right back." She opened a door and let herself into the bathroom.

After what seemed like an eternity, Galina slipped back into the room, shutting the door behind her quietly. She was gloriously naked and he, as promised, was undressed and waiting. She came slowly towards him, each delicious step increasing his ardour. He was grunting quite loudly by now.

As she reached the couch, she launched herself and smeared all over him.

"Oh my god," breathed Shri Vindaloo loudly as their bodies caressed each other.

"Softly," whispered Galina but she became more and more voluble herself. Shri Vindaloo's eyes were closed but he saw her lovely lips, eyes, hair; Galina was almost acrobatic atop him and suddenly –

A loud CRACK and the sofa collapsed beneath them.

The door to the ante-chamber burst open and Masha, a man with a tea tray following a respectable distance behind, rushed in. "What happened? [in Russian]"

Shri Vindaloo and Galina were lying naked, half on the sofa and half on the floor. Laughing, Galina rolled off him, "[in Russian] Masha, what can I say?"

"[in Russian] Galya, what will I tell the President?" And then, she, too, began to laugh at the tableau, with Shri Vindaloo still half-on the sofa, completely naked and

Galina, with her hand on his thigh near him on the floor, also naked.

"[in Russian] Tell him Shri Vindaloo fell ill; tell him I'll tell his wife; tell him anything."

Masha said, "Get dressed both of you." Turning to the tea boy, she said something sternly in Russian; he turned tail and left the room.

Galina went into the bathroom and Shri Vindaloo looked for his clothes, which were just by Masha's feet. As he reached to retrieve them, she leaned down to help him, brushing against his naked body.

She smiled at him and left to join Galina in the bathroom.

He heard them talking to each other in Russian, laughing from time to time. When they came out, Masha left the room and Galina came up to Shri Vindaloo and kissed him tenderly, "Shri Vindaloo, you will have to go back to India now."

"Now?" They were just getting to know each other.

"Masha will make all the arrangements. Comrade Korovski will take you back to the hotel but we won't be able to see each other again."

"But... but we just met," pulling her to him. "We can't just end like this."

"Shri Vindaloo, I love you. But love in Leningrad is sometimes like this. But I will have your coconuts to play with to keep me happy. And you..." She kissed him for what seemed like forever. "And you will keep that with you for a long time."

"Forever, Galina," said Shri Vindaloo, holding her close.

By this time, Andrei and Masha had come in. They all made more formal goodbyes and Andrei escorted Shri Vindaloo down in the lift. It was clear that he didn't know what had happened and, equally clearly, he didn't know where to begin to find out. They tromped through the hotel lobby in silence, although Shri Vindaloo did proffer a few waves to occasional pigs who nodded at him.

The lady pig driver was also more than curious and she jumped out of the car to open the door for Shri Vindaloo. Andrei got in silently, "Hotel, Comrade."

Shri Vindaloo enjoyed the last of Leningrad on the drive in a post-not-quite-coital haze. "Amazing city," he said to nobody in particular.

"Yes."

When they arrived at the hotel, Andrei was more energized, but still silent and had his usual strong grip on Shri Vindaloo's arm. He ushered Shri Vindaloo into the elevator, up to the 13th floor, past an even more frightening-looking dezhurnaya and into his room.

As soon as the door was shut, Andrei became extremely apologetic. "Shree Vendaloo, I am really, really sorry. I don't know what happened in the President's office but I have instructions to lock you inside your room till your flight is ready."

"Oh, Andrei, it was wonderful."

"What was wonderful, Shree Vendaloo?"

He was never one to kiss and tell, but the adventure was so extraordinary and strangely joyous that he pulled out Galina's letter that started it all and handed it to Andrei.

Andrei read it in amazement and with increasing joy. "But, but...why are you leaving?"

"Love in Leningrad, my dear Andrei, I am told, is sometimes like that."

"Ah, Shree Vendaloo, you are ... what can I say? But, I must report downstairs immediately. There is vodka – two bottles – and ice and the best Russian chocolates I could find. And, the hotel has arranged a Raj Kapoor movie on the television. I hope you will be comfortable."

Shri Vindaloo poured himself a large vodka, knocked it back and poured another one, which he filled with ice and sat on the sofa by the television. He thought about Galina and her whispering kisses, he thought about her soft... "Ahhhh....," he sighed.

He reached for some chocolates and the remote and turned on the TV. And, wouldn't you know, the movie they had cued up for him was "Bobby."

Shri Vindaloo loved the movie and with a few more vodkas, he slowly drifted off into a dreamy sleep. Galina, Galina, Galina!

He was awakened again by Andrei. But something was different. This Andrei was smiling, happy even. And Shri Vindaloo saw that he had replaced his usual colourless tie with the snappy one Shri Vindaloo had given him – it was orange and gold and green and really suited him.

"You look so handsome, Andrei."

"Thank you, Shri Vindaloo. But, we must leave now."

"But not before..." Shri Vindaloo poured two large vodkas, which they toasted and knocked back. Andrei rushed about packing Shri Vindaloo's effects and, by the time they had toasted another vodka, they were out the door.

Wonder of wonders, the dezhurnaya was smiling, and raised her arm in a farewell greeting. The lift smelled sweet and in the lobby it was almost like the entire staff had lined up to say goodbye – including, to his delight, Valentina, who once again pressed her body to his, "You wish sex?"

He didn't want to turn her down again, but again efficient – and brighter – Andrei steered him out the door into the car, where the lady driver looked even lovelier that usual. "How smart you look Shri Vindaloo," the first words she had said since he arrived.

Andrei, more gently than usual, said, "To the airport, comrade."

On the way to the airport, Andrei turned positively garrulous. He told Shri Vindaloo about his parents and also Anya, the delightful young pig he had fallen in love with but couldn't pursue because...well, just because. "But now, thanks to you, Shri Vindaloo, I will find my Anya."

At the airport, the car was waved directly to the tarmac where a smallish jet was waiting. Andrei embraced Shri Vindaloo and chivvied him up the steps, as the driver girl tried to offer her greetings as well. Once on the plane, Shri Vindaloo discovered that he was the only passenger.

A tall, statuesque pig, dressed like a Western fashion model, greeted him, "Welcome Shri Vindaloo."

"Masha?" said Shri Vindaloo, amazed and delighted.

"No, I am Svetlana," she said in an attractive, low voice. "I am Masha's sister."

"Twins?"

She nodded. "Masha asked me to give you this note. And let me get you some champagne."

Shri Vindaloo recognized Galina's handwriting. And in any case, it was addressed to MY PRECIOUS ANGEL. She wrote how happy she was to meet him, he was everything and more than she remembered and now she had their interrupted liaison to remember as well.

Shri Vindaloo settled into the plush seat. Svetlana brought his champagne and said, "Masha told me to make sure you get everything you desire."

He smiled and fastened his seat belt.

Easter Parade

It was Easter Sunday and the surf was up. Shri Vindaloo hopped up the three stairs to his terrace, shielding his eyes with his plump paw. He could hear the seagulls cawing over the sound of the surf, and somewhere, in the silences between their raucous cries, it sounded like The Beach Boys wailing one of his favourite songs: Surfer Girl.

His thoughts immediately sped to another Easter Sunday a decade or two earlier, when he was a young buck pig, strutting out each evening on the promenade – tight jeans, puff brightly pomaded, red neckerchief fluttering casually in the breeze. How handsome Master Vindaloo looks, the mama pigs whispered to each other behind their fans, secretly scheming to get him to dance with their marriageable young girl pigs.

For even then – long before he had earned the sobriquet Shri Vindaloo – he was a renowned dancer. He threw his large snout back and clicked his hooves in time to the music when the band played up-tempo ballads and his eyes sparkled when it shifted to those romantic Konkani love songs.

The Easter he was remembering, though, was a turning point – the day the music changed.

A strange and lovely young lady pig of indeterminate age and origin strolled into the Easter service, wearing a shockingly short, brilliant yellow dress – mango-coloured, thought Master Vindaloo, but that may have been the ripening mango season. Instead of carrying a fan she wore a huge-brimmed straw hat, which, of course, she swept off her head as she entered the church and sat down next to him.

She smiled sweetly at him, and, indeed, the entire congregation, all of whom had NOTICED her all right. The pig pastor, who was a modern sort, smiled her a welcome. In fact, and maybe as a result of the beauty sitting by him, the Easter sermon was a little livelier than usual, Master Vindaloo thought.

At the end of the service, she stepped out of church, almost leading Master Vindaloo by the snout. She turned to him and snapped on a transistor radio she had been clutching out of sight in her purse.

A loud burst of music exploded in the churchyard, surprising the post-service congregation, who were sniffing around for the usual coconut water and snacks. Master Vindaloo, a gentleman before his years, bowed to the lady pig and held out his paw.

She smiled, winking at him and set the radio down on the topmost church step. He did a grand pirouette, spinning the light-footed girl pig clockwise and anti. She pulled back from him calling out "Surf" repeatedly as she snaked her front paws up and down in a motion reminiscent of the waves. Master Vindaloo was amazed – the radio was playing a song called Surfs Up, by the Beach Boys. He had never heard it before, but that day it seemed as if he had written it himself.

He grunted in rhythm and, before long, the entire congregation, including the pig ladies who were serving coconut water, were juked up. Music and dancing were like fresh air to the pigs – and over the after-service session, several coconuts ended up rolling wildly around the churchyard. It was an Easter to remember and since then, the shapely blond pig – Nishasha was her name – was folded warmly into the village bosom.

She was a "beauty consultant" and set up a salon in a small shack on the beach that Master Vindaloo – my Easter Piggy, she called him – found for her. She had two chairs for her customers, both yellow, one of which reclined permanently and the other which spun around rather idiosyncratically, sometimes resulting in abstract haircut patterns. She offered her special hair care and manipedi, and also did tattoos, which had some of the village pig ladies a little concerned for their sons, many of whom, made a pig line outside the salon most afternoons after school, ostensibly to listen to the never-ending music that came from the place, but also to catch a glimpse of Nishasha, who was often a little risqué in her dress.

Easter Piggy, of course, spent a lot of time around the salon, bringing her cool drinks, fanning her when the afternoons grew too hot, and, in the evenings, dancing with her and sometimes her customers out onto the beach. She introduced him to Bob Dylan and Frank Sinatra and the Beatles and the Rolling Stones – she often teased him, *You can't always get what you want, Easter Piggy.*

Of course, Nishasha lavished care above and beyond the call of beauty on Master Vindaloo – manicuring his hooves, shaving his noble jowls and keeping his fuzz trimmed in various fashionable designs, to a point where he often – certainly from behind – looked like an Easter egg. There were other ministrations, of course, particularly as Master Vindaloo was coming of age.

And, in what seemed like a twinkling of an eye, more and more people, including the pastor of the church took to calling him Shri Vindaloo.

And one day, suddenly, Nishasha disappeared. Shri Vindaloo had sauntered over to the salon around noon and, to his curious surprise, it was quiet. The music was always on at the salon, even when she was asleep, and you could hear it through the surf and the bird calls all the way down the beach.

But that day, it was silent. He opened the door and found a couple of chickens perched on the reclining chair and on the big mirror was a note written in lipstick outlined with a big heart. She had to go to New York, she said; it was almost Easter and it was said there was a magnificent parade there every Easter and her Easter Piggy must visit her there.

And she had left him a gift, of course: a large box of coconuts, each one shaved and trimmed delicately to resemble his own most beautifully-crafted Easter egg head.

Shri Vindaloo scratched his noble jaw and his egghead thinking. "Ah Nishisha," he said aloud and somewhere in the back of his mind he tucked a reminder – New York Easter Parade.

Several years later, on the day before Easter, Shri Vindaloo took off for New York by boat, train and aeroplane. Nishisha met him at Kennedy Airport and my, how changed she looked – even more attractive than he remembered and with a certain... a certain urbaneness to her. Her skirts were short, as always, but her make-up was stranger, darker in a way and her manner, too, had become more My Way than Whatever. And she had become a bit fuller, he thought, even more delicious than he remembered.

As she folded him in her now-almost ample bosom, she said, "We must have Manhattans", and led him, a little jet-lagged, into an elevator which delivered them to a terrace overlooking the tarmac, with planes taking off and landing every few minutes.

She called to the waiter with her usual "I own this place" smiling attitude and forthwith they were delivered two deep, dark cocktails, which were beyond delicious. Shri Vindaloo had, till then, favoured cashew feni with soda, which brought the sun out from behind his eyes and sprouted more and more hair on his chest. But there was no sun in New York (it was night) and the Manhattans were – as he sat paw in paw with Nishasha – every bit as wonderful.

They had a few Manhattans and Nishasha regaled him with tales he couldn't quite understand and, as the jet lag got stronger, he found himself yawning and yawning. Nishasha saw this too and quickly, shushing his attempts to pay the bill, bundled him into the elevator and into a taxicab which sped into the city.

And, my word. New York was New York was New York. Shri Vindaloo's jet lag vanished and his amazed snout hung out of the window all the way into town watching the city and its twinkling lights and its madness, as Nishasha chattered on with the cabdriver. She was telling him that her friend, Easter Piggy, had flown in all the way from Goa to go to the Easter Parade with her and that she had to get to her place on Elizabeth Street quickly as she was late to get somewhere. The cabbie said, "If you ain't late, you ain't in New York" and put his foot to the floor.

When they landed – it had felt like another airplane ride – Shri Vindaloo thanked the cab driver in his usual old-fashioned way, smiling and bowing and, indeed, skipping on the uneven pavement. Nishasha scurried him into a narrow doorway and up three flights of stairs – fortunately, he travelled light – and flung open the door to her apartment – ta da!

He was exhausted and she laid him down on her bed; his head was spinning a bit and he saw multiple visions in her house including a few pictures from the old salon in Goa and a box full of coconuts, ready to be shaved.

"My salon's downstairs," she said. "And your Easter outfit is ready. But I must be off. I'll come for you at 7:30 tomorrow morning!" And completing his confusion with a profusion of soft, wet kisses, she was gone.

It was late, he was tired, the room had an intoxicating fragrance and before long, Shri Vindaloo was snoring happily. He dreamt of a mishmash of pig girls he had loved and loved still, and in the dream they began to look more and more like Nishasha, who was clicking a pair of scissors about his head in time to a mambo. I love New York, he mumbled in his sleep and turned over and around in the narrow bed.

Suddenly, it was morning and Nishisha was sitting on the edge of the bed running her fingers through the hair on his chest. "Easter Piggy," she whispered, "we have to go. The parade has started and ..."

Shri Vindaloo jumped up, "Parade! When? Where are the floats?" He remembered going to the carnival parades in Goa every year since he was a small pig, and, even today, he remembered the bright, sweet and (sometimes) mad decorations of the floats from earlier years. And one year – the year after Nishasha had come to Goa, he recalled – he had been made the King of the Carnaval.

Nishasha had a cup of coconut-flavoured coffee for him and said, "We must go downstairs and dress."

He didn't like to rush in the morning, but this was New York, he figured. And this was Nishisha. She had the front door open and they almost flew down the stairs to her salon. And there, to his delight, he found that she had almost reconstructed the Goa salon, complete with mismatched chairs and, amazingly, two chickens. She pushed a button near the door and the music started.

"Come, Easter Piggy," she said leading him to the armoire, from which she extracted a gorgeous egg-yolk yellow pair of trousers. He was still in his travel clothes, which he threw to the floor and pulled on the remarkable breeches, preening in the mirror. "It's Easter," he said, "it's perfect. Let's go!"

"But wait," she said. She knew that Shri Vindaloo liked to live bare-chested but it was cold in New York so she had fashioned an Easter-cape that would give him some coverage but enable him to easily shuck it off if it got too warm. The cape was emblazoned with a pattern of fried eggs and chocolate macaroons. She had also fashioned a "thislittlepiggywenttomarket" kind of sailor cap for him with orange and yellow and gold streamers. When he put it all of it on, he looked good enough to eat.

She quickly slipped into a very svelte Easter dress – Shri Vindaloo hmm'd again that she had become quite the pig woman – this one in, of all colors, black but with hundreds of multi-coloured coconuts dancing all over. Her bonnet was coconut shaped as well, with the same orange and yellow and gold streamers. She was in New York but she was remembering Goa.

She grabbed his paw and out the door. "We must rush. The parade has started and…"

"Where are the floats," bleated Shri Vindaloo.

"Easter Piggy, there are no floats. The people are the parade and you, my darling, look like the Queen of the Easter Parade."

"No floats, how could that be? The people are the parade, whatever do you mean? And you did mean King, didn't you?" Shri Vindaloo rattled on as she dragged him into a cab and they were on the way.

"Grand Central Station please," Nishisha squealed as they got in.

"You guys look like breakfast," said the cabbie. "I guess you're going to the Easter Parade."

Shri Vindaloo, paw in paw with Nishisha, had his snout out the window again enjoying the sights and smells and sounds of Manhattan.

He turned to her, "This is amazing," in an unusual singsong.

"We'll be meeting some friends in the park," she said tentatively but he was out the window again.

"Great!" for he was a sociable type.

"Including Oilypig," she said tentatively.

"Great – look at that!" Shri Vindaloo was turning into Mister New York.

"He's a special friend" she said, a little quietly.

"Great – huh," He brought himself back into the cab. "Special?"

"Well," she continued hurriedly, "He's exactly the opposite of you, Easter Piggy. You'll love him."

"Special?" he said again, this time in a smaller voice.

"Well, you know darling, it's been a long time since I came here and…and Oilypig and I are leaving for Senegal tomorrow."

"Senegal? Isn't that in Africa somewhere?"

By then, the cab had stopped in front of an impressive building with people, people, people everywhere rushing past each other. So, this is what she meant – the people are the parade.

Nishisha tucked him under her arm and guided him through the crowds on 42nd Street. It wasn't an easy task for Shri Vindaloo was very easily sidetracked, particularly in a grand entertainment like New York. But she pulled and tugged him forward till they got to the corner of 42nd and 5th – they almost tumbled into the centre of the street and Shri Vindaloo whooped aloud as he saw sights that overwhelmed his in-any-case-delighted eyes. Everybody was so wonderfully dressed in all sort of silly colours with eggs and bunnies and baskets on their heads; there were pig couples with babies and pigs with dogs and pig ladies with green hair and pig men with frogs jumping out of their snouts and....

And, of course, Shri Vindaloo and Nishisha were (as the say) the cynosure of all eyes. People kept photographing them, smiling at them, singing at them, sometimes even kissing them. A child tried to eat one of the chocolate macaroons on Shri Vindaloo's cape and, wonder of wonders, it was real chocolate. How had Nishisha made this?

She was so open and free and as he traipsed beside, behind, alongside her, it was as if they knew everybody in the parade.

And, before long, they were at the park. There were hundreds – no, thousands – of pigs there, and even though it was much less crowded than the parade, it looked like the trees and the bushes and the trees and the small lakes were all dressed up for Easter too.

"Welcome to New York," sang Nishisha sillily, and led him scampering straight through the meandering crowds to a little hillock a short way into the park, to a group of pigs lying on the grass and chitchatting.

"And, here we are! Easter Piggy, this is Oilypig." He was a rather large pig with pink eyeglasses. She took his paw. "Oilypig, this is Easter Piggy from Goa, who I told you about."

"I've never been to Goa," said Oilypig. "I've been all over India but never to Goa."

"Oh, you must come," said Shri Vindaloo. "Goa is one of two places that everybody in the world loves. The other, of course, is Italy."

"I've never been to Italy, either. But we're going to Senegal tomorrow"

Nishisha had sauntered off and brought a few other pigs to introduce Easter Piggy. They all ooh-ed and aah-ed at him and, of course, his Easter regalia, and then subsided back to the grass, where they were smoking pot.

The joint came around to Shri Vindaloo who took a tentative puff and started coughing. "Here," said Oilypig, "let me help you." He took a deep drag on the joint and then kissed Shri Vindaloo on the lips and released a delicious smoke into his chest.

"Mmmmm," thought Shri Vindaloo and, suddenly, found himself laughing.

Oilypig was laughing, too, and they continued work on the joint and chitted and laughed and chatted and laughed, and before long, they were like they had been best friends from childhood.

Oilypig was from London and had spent a lot of time in India. He had met Nishisha just as she left Goa that year to go to New York. He had built a motorized cycle rickshaw that he was riding to Madras and, of course, Nishisha joined him as pillion.

While he told Shri Vindaloo some stories of their ride, Nishisha joined them and all three of them just laughed and smoked and made silly faces at the world. Suddenly, Oilypig slipped away. They saw him rushing to a cluster of bushes – perhaps, he had business.

"See, Easter Piggy, I told you that you'd love Oilypig. He's quite mad and quite wonderful. But sometimes he gets very serious, despite his pink glasses. And actually, he's not like you at all. But, I love him and I love you Easter Piggy and I'm so happy to see you. But, we – Oilypig and I – have to leave for Senegal now."

"Now," squeaked Shri Vindaloo.

"But don't you worry. You stay in my apartment as long as you like and I have arranged for three of my friends," she pointed to a trio of pretty young lady pigs, dressed as different Easter candies and smiling at him, "who will take care of you for as long as you are in New York."

Shri Vindaloo bowed, kissed Nishisha tenderly and, as she scurried away to find Oilypig, made his way, licking his lips, to the Candy Store.

Cowboy P'lite

Shri Vindaloo woke rather late in the day clutching at memories of the previous night that swirled through his smiling brain. He remembered that all three of Nishisha's friends – Pigbeauty, LovelyPig and Pigjoy – had spent the night in the crowded apartment with him but they were all gone and he couldn't remember much of anything else. The previous two or three weeks had been a swirl of parties, drinking and smoking and dancing with pig ladies and pig men and some who could have been both or either. "This is downtown, y'know," Pigjoy had cackled.

He got out of the rumpled bed and, after a not too satisfactory visit to the facilities, opened the refrigerator. There was a slightly stale Entenmann's Danish, a very stale poppy seed bagel and a half-finished carton of orange juice. Not the standard breakfast at Pig Enterprises.

New York is New York, he said aloud, but I must go home.

LovelyPig – he thought it was – had told him there was an airline ticket office just outside Grand Central station so he hit the streets sniffing around, nodding to everyone and smiling at all the pig girls he passed, even the ones with colored hair. After wandering for what seemed like a week, he got to a subway station by late afternoon. He asked the token seller how he could get to Grand Central; she grunted "Number 6" and gesticulated with her very large head towards a platform behind him.

Shri Vindaloo trotted onto the train still smiling at everyone. At first, he was a bit surprised that people didn't smile back, despite his tight pompadour and gold shades; but then, realizing that nobody seemed to even notice him, he hmmd, *Maybe I'm becoming a New Yorker*.

After a few stops, he heard the scratchy PA system announce "Grand Central Station, change for…". The rest was drowned out as he was carried off the train onto the platform. He had to scamper to avoid being run over but he kept up with the crowd that flowed with remarkable purpose towards and up an escalator and then through a maze of corridors and then, suddenly, POOF! He found himself in a temple.

It was quite unlike any temple he had ever seen – it had a towering Beaux-Arts dome whose roof was covered with the stars of the zodiac; there were cathedral-type windows on one end with a religious light streaming through; there was this extraordinary clock right in the centre, which made him realize it was a temple of time. But, other than a few lost-looking souls, there was nobody praying.

There were, of course, pigs, pigs, pigs, a whirlpool of pigs of all shapes and sizes and colours and sexes and who-knows-what rushing to who-knows-where. He staggered around transfixed, looking at the ceiling, looking at the pigs, looking at the clock – it was five o'clock. He was feeling giddy and open-mouthed, he tried to slow down the spinning.

And suddenly, BAM!

He found himself on the floor with a gorgeous pig looking annoyedly down at him. He hadn't seen her coming and had run right into her, it seems, and as he fumblingly apologized, she helped him up apologizing as well. She smiled at him, Are you OK? Her lipstick was blinding. He nodded, I'm sorry. No, *I'm* sorry, but I have to run, and she was off.

Welcome to New York.

He was still disoriented and, unsurprisingly, found that he was thirsty. Looking around, a cocktail bar on the upper concourse called to him. He trotted up, rubbing his knee where the beauty's briefcase had bumped him, and waited to be seated. The hostess pig smiled him over to a table at the parapet overlooking the main concourse. The waiter was right behind her and he was about to order a Manhattan, when the waiter said he should try one of their Old Fashioneds – he'd like it.

He sat back surveying the continuing performance on the concourse, and when his drink arrived, he took a large sip, and applauding loudly, thanked the waiter. It was perfect!

Smiling around the bar, he noticed a beautiful pig sitting at the very next table. She was looking straight at him, with a twinkle in here eye; she said, "I saw you get knocked down on the concourse; are you alright?"

"Oh yes, nothing to it," he waved his arms about. "Can I buy you a drink?"

"Why, thank you," she said. He rose, crossing to her table, and offered her his paw back to his table. The excellent waiter quickly brought her drink across.

"What are you drinking?" he asked her.

"Tequila sunrise," she said. "You?"

"An Old Fashioned – a very elegant cocktail, I might add."

"You do look like an old fashioned kind of guy. But," she quickly added, "in the best possible way."

"Well, thank you. This is my first Old Fashioned ever. I just got to New York a few days ago and the only cocktail I knew was a Manhattan, but now…"

"Welcome to New York. My name's Patty and I'm from California."

"California!" said Shri Vindaloo, "My name is Shri Vindaloo and I'm from Goa. In India"

"My god, that's pretty far away. So, what brings you to New York, Shri Vindaloo from Goa?"

"I came here for the Easter Parade and to see my friend Nishisha." He looked around at the waiter just a bit from his shoulder. "Can we get two more of these, please?"

He turned back to Patty who said, "Is Nishisha your girlfriend?"

"Well," Shri Vindaloo pinked a little. "Yes and no. She had to leave for Senegal with Oilypig the next day but she gave me the keys to her apartment and three of her friends have been taking such wonderful care of me for the past week or two or three."

"Lucky pig," she said, as the drinks arrived. "But now," switching glasses, "you have the Tequila Sunrise and I'll have the Old Fashioned."

"That's a great idea," said Shri Vindaloo, taking a long sip. "Oooh, that's really lovely! It reminds me a bit of feni."

"What's feni?"

"Feni is a magical drink from Goa."

"Magical? Like how?"

"Well," said Shri Vindaloo, "you know if you drink a lot of anything – say, whiskey – you get drunk. But if you drink a lot of feni, you *do* get drunk but... you also see GOD."

His voice had risen an octave or two. Several people in the bar turn to look at them.

"I haven't seen God in a long time," she said.

"But," he continued, looking straight at her demure chest, "it may not work for you."

"Why not?"

"Well, it also grows hair on your chest." He undoes one more button on his shirt. "See?"

"I think I'll pass on the feni, in that case," she said, smiling at him and taking another sip of her Old Fashioned.

"So, what brings you to New York?"

"I've just written a book and my publisher is here in New York."

"That's pretty impressive," said Shri Vindaloo. "Congratulations! And what is the book about?"

"Two pigs who meet in a bar," she laughs. "Give me your address in Goa and I'll send you an autographed copy when its released."

"That would be perfect," said Shri Vindaloo clapping his paws, and downing the rest of his Tequila Sunrise. "I think we need two more to celebrate your book."

"Of course," said Patty. "But I'm catching a flight back to the coast tonight so ...."

"You're leaving tonight? But we just met.."

"Well, you'll just have to come and see me in California, won't you, Shri Vindaloo?"

"I certainly will. But in the meantime, we should go out on the town, as they say, in New York."

"Let's down our drinks and blow this joint."

He looked around for the check and by the time he had settled up, the waiter had an even broader smile, and Patty and Shri Vindaloo were arm in arm down to the concourse, out on the street and into a cab in no time at all.

She said South something-or-another to the cab driver, and they settled in quite close to each other, talking sometimes at the same time, pointing out things to each other, their knees and paws and sometimes other parts touching from time to time. It was getting romantic.

When the cab stopped, she dragged him into the terminal. "This is the most romantic place in New York," she said dreamily.

He had no idea what this was, but he was already happy to follow her anywhere. They went to the upper deck just as the ferry was pulling out of Manhattan and WOW!

The lights of the skyscrapers downtown made his heart blink with delight. She pulled him to the railing and kissed him in a way that made him forget even that. "Let's smoke a joint," she said, pulling one out of her shirt pocket.

Since the Easter Parade, Shri Vindaloo had developed something of a taste for pot – he found it made him even happier than he always was, and sometimes it made him feel like a kitten. He must be careful not to fall off the boat.

They sat close together on the deck and held hands and held each other and kissed and smoked the joint and...Shri Vindaloo felt like he was falling in love.

"I'm starved." Patty said suddenly, jumping up and dragging him to the café counter. They got beers and hotdogs; his with mustard and hers with everything – mustard, sauerkraut and God knows what else. He took a tentative bite, savouring the taste; she just jammed almost the whole thing into her mouth greedily, smiling and grunting, her pretty face turned into a composition in sauerkraut. They laughed and sipped their beers; she kissed him again getting sauerkraut and stuff all over him too.

"I think I love you, Patty Pig. I know I love you with sauerkraut."

She laughed, handing him a stack of paper towels. They kissed and canoodled some more and, of course, wrote each other's addresses and phone numbers on the ragged paper towels. And, too soon, the ferry grated its way back into the terminal.

She pulled back from their embrace and looked at her watch. "I hate to kiss and run, darlin' but I have to leave for the airport RIGHT NOW." She smiled, "Come and see me in California."

"I'll come tomorrow," he said immediately.

She thought for a while and said, "No, no, not tomorrow. I'll need a day to settle down. Why don't you come the day after – there's a United flight leaving La Guardia at 10 in the morning which gets to LA around noon and then you can catch the 115 Greyhound to Needles. I'll be there to get you."

"Needles?"

"That's the closest big town to where I live. I'll collect you and we'll drive to my place in the desert."

"You live in the desert? That's amazing – I've never been to the desert," said Shri Vindaloo, almost jumping up and down.

They got off the ferry hand in hand and played another deliciously romantic scene at the taxi line and suddenly, with a hasta la vista, baby, she was gone.

Shri Vindaloo sank in delicious confusion into the back seat of his cab, and gave the driver his – Nishisha's – home address.

"Goodbyes are tough, ain't they," said the cabbie, who had been watching their movie at the terminal.

"This was both hello and goodbye," said Shri Vindaloo, "but who knows? Maybe not."

"Who knows," said the philosopher and both of them went their own dreamy ways. "Good luck," he told Shri Vindaloo, stopping the cab at the house.

"Thank you, my friend."

Shri Vindaloo slept fitfully that night, dreaming of Patty, naked, reading to him in the desert.

First thing in the morning, he got a nice breakfast from the bodega downstairs – barter bagel and a regular coffee to go – and took a cab to the airline ticket office outside Grand Central. He had called Eunice Pig before he went to sleep and, of course, his ticket was waiting for him.

After he picked it up, he walked – cool as ever – through Grand Central, up past the cocktail bar and out the side entrance to get to Fifth Avenue. He had to go shopping. For Eunice Pig, of course; she took such good care of him. She had also suggested and booked him an open dated ticket back to Goa from Los Angeles – he was missing home but he didn't know how long he'd be in the desert with Patty. And he also wanted to get gifts for Pigbeauty and LovelyPig and PigJoy, who had taken such delighted care of him. And, of course, for Nishisha, without whom none of this would have happened. For Patty… well he hoped he'd be gift enough.

He walked up Fifth Avenue nodding at the various small storefronts till he came to Saks Fifth Avenue. He had heard of it and strode in expectantly through the revolving doors, but was met with a revoltingly sweet smell. He simply turned around and strode out again. Whatever was that smell?

Right next door there was the very grand St. Patrick's Cathedral. He walked in, much more at home – Goa had hundreds of churches and dozens of cathedrals, and even though Shri Vindaloo was not devout, in the usual sense, he delighted in the real fervour you sometimes felt in real houses of worship. He walked around the cathedral gazing uncritically at the architecture and smiling at the hordes of tourists, all of whom seemed to be unnecessarily sombre.

He thought to himself, God doesn't need you to be sombre, God needs you to be happy.

He made a quiet exit and, stepping into the sunlight, saw Atlas, the founder of astronomy, standing astride his globe across the avenue. He wanted to speak with him, but crossing Fifth Avenue felt like taking his life into his hands, so he simply waved and continued uptown from the cathedral.

There were several other large stores but the only one that really caught his eye was the window at FAO Schwarz. There was a large pink dog moving its head from left to right, right to left, and smiling at him. Happy at the invitation, he wandered in and was immediately overwhelmed with small pigs running about amid a huge display of very large toys and boxes. He ventured carefully further in, and he was suddenly struck dumb: he saw himself, slender as a reed. He couldn't believe it; he took a couple of steps to one side and, my God, he was suddenly as big as a blimp.

A pretty salesgirl pig, seeing his delighted consternation, came up to him and said, "It's a funhouse mirror."

"I want it," said Shri Vindaloo, imagining it in Nishisha's salon behind the chairs; her clients would have so much fun they'd never leave.

"I'm sorry sir, it's for our display. It's not for sale."

"But I must have it," said Shri Vindaloo, looking around.

"Oh, Shri Vindaloo, welcome to FAO Schwarz," said a smartly-dressed manager pig.

Shri Vindaloo was startled. "You know me?"

"Yes, of course. We saw you at the Easter Parade and they even had pictures of you on TV, your Easter cape was so striking."

"Well, thank you, Mister…"

"Porker. I'm PigPorker, manager of the store," putting out his well-manicured paw.

Shri Vindaloo took his paw. "It's such a delight to meet you. Wasn't the Easter Parade magical?"

"Yes. And I'm blessed. I get to see it first-hand every year."

"You are a lucky pig, indeed. I must return to it again."

"Mr. Porker," the salesgirl pig stuck her pretty snout into the conversation. "Shri Vindaloo wanted the funhouse mirror, and I was telling him…"

"Well, I'm sure we can get him a new one from the warehouse in New Jersey. Where would you like us to have it delivered, Shri Vindaloo?"

Shri Vindaloo explained that it was a gift for a friend, except she was out of the country – in Senegal – but he would get one of her friends to call Mr. Porker and explain where they needed it delivered. Mr. Porker handed him a business card and the pretty salesgirl pig asked for his autograph.

They were all so helpful. He smiled and thanked them and, beaming across the entire salesroom, stepped out to cries of "Come back and see us soon, Shri Vindaloo."

That was nice, he thought. New York is so friendly, particularly when you are spending money. He was caught up in a flow of pigs across the street to Central Park and the Plaza Hotel. He thought he should perhaps stop for a libation, but he had to take care of business – he hadn't yet seen anything for the other pig girls and ladies who had all taken such good care of him.

He walked a couple of blocks down Fifth Avenue, looking left and right down each of the cross streets, and on 57th street, he saw a store window in the middle of the block that seemed alight with delight. He crossed the street and walked over – it was Henri Bendel's and the window was glowing because of these extravagantly decorated necklaces. There were, by a nice coincidence, four of them, made of enamel with some very pretty stones, each with a fruit motif – one was banana, another was apple, the third was pineapple and the fourth, of course, was coconut.

He went into the store and said, aloud, "I want the four necklaces in the window."

Three or four pigs surrounded him and patted and coddled him as one of them got the necklaces, two of them set to packing them – individually, please – and the fourth, again, took his autograph. *They must have seen me at the Easter Parade as well.*

A little tired from all the shopping, Shri Vindaloo thanked them as one of them hailed him a taxi.

He got back to the apartment, thinking he would rest awhile and call the pig girls so he could give them their gifts. But, surprise – they were all there already, neatening up the place. They had made the bed and washed the dishes and had even stocked the refrigerator, including a bottle of tequila in the freezer.

"Darlings," said Shri Vindaloo, "how wonderful to see you and how thoughtful of you to do all this."

"Shri Vindaloo," they started up almost in chorus. One of them, Pigjoy, jumped the line and kissed him with the others following. "There's a party tonight," said Lovelypig. "We must go."

"I have to go to California and the flight leaves quite early tomorrow." It was very difficult for Shri Vindaloo to decline a party.

"Oh, but it'll be great."

"You'll love it."

"We'll get back early. But, what's in California?"

"Well, I met this girl…"

"Great, bring her to the party."

"She left last night."

"Oh… are you in love with her?"

"I don't know…I think so."

"That's fantastic, Shri Vindaloo. But that's all the more reason to come to the party," this was Pigbeauty.

"Well, for a little while… but, I have something for each of you." He gave the banana necklace to Pigjoy, the apple one to Lovelypig and the pineapple to Pigbeauty.

"These are beautiful, thank you Shri Vindaloo."

"They're just lovely."

"What a joy!"

"And, I need you to do me a favour," taking out Porkerpig's business card. "You have to call this man who will be delivering a grand and strange mirror for Nishisha and set it up behind the chairs in the salon before she returns from Senegal."

"You are so thoughtful, Shri Vindaloo."

"Let's have shots of tequila and then …"

"How did you know I liked tequila?"

"Shri Vindaloo, you love everything."

"Nazdorovia!"

And they went on and out to the party and Shri Vindaloo was escorted home about 2 am. He kissed the girls and made them cry when he said goodbye.

"Hasta la vista, darlings."

He had never been to LA before but had heard wondrous things about 24-hour sunshine, pink cocktails and sexy movie stars everywhere. And he wasn't disappointed.

He was greeted on the tarmac by a pink convertible Cadillac driven by a voluptuous blonde pig girl; she was wearing a pink bikini kind of thing and air-kissed him as she waved him into the back seat. "Greyhound terminal, right?" she sang, and before he could answer, she gunned the car and took off.

He tried, in his most suave way, to make conversation – she was quite a beauty. But she couldn't hear him; she had the radio on full volume and was sashaying around bouncing to the beat. There was a pair of pink-tinted shades on the seat, which fit perfectly on his head.

Catching his eye in the rear-view mirror, she singsonged at him," There's margaritas in the mini-fridge, handsome."

He opened the mini-fridge to a tray with a cocktail shaker and a chilled martini glass. Balanced between the cocktail shaker and the martini glass was a company brochure promoting a body shaping salon, with a picture of a tanned and tip-top surfing couple; he suddenly remembered "Surfer Girl" by the Beach Boys. He turned the picture over to a message

WELCOME TO LA, SHRI VINDALOO

COME BACK WHEN YOU CAN STAY WITH ME A WHILE

LOVE (with lipstick marks)

MONELLA

Of course, Monella! Madame Olga's daughter! She had moved to Los Angeles some years ago and Eunice Pig must have called her about his visit.

He smiled and poured himself a drink and – wouldn't you know it – it was pink. He took a sip – it tasted of sunshine. And reminded him strangely of the drinks he had had with Patty.

Just perfect, he thought, falling back into the cushions, enjoying his margarita and dozing despite the thump-throbbing music.

An hour or so later, the limousine pulled up outside the Greyhound terminal, and the pink pig chauffeuress ran around to the passenger door, handed him a huge bouquet of pink roses, and sent him off with a delicious moist kiss. "Happy trails", she sang and charged off.

Shri Vindaloo scratched his head and rubbed his lips, staggering into the bus station. "One way to Needles, please," he said, smiling at the tired-looking pig lady at the ticket counter. She laughed out loud, pointing at the smudged lipstick on his face.

"Well," he said, "welcome to Los Angeles."

She made change and handed over his ticket. "The bus leaves in seven minutes," she said.

He got on the bus and, delighted and exhausted from the flight and the margaritas, fell asleep, still wearing his pink shades and carrying the bouquet of pink roses. He dreamed of Patty, who now looked like a combination of Monella and the sexy young pig who drove him to the bus station. He snorted quietly, singing in his sleep.

Four and a half hours later, he was awakened by the screeching brakes of the bus. It was late afternoon and hot, hot, hot deep in the desert.

He struggled off the bus and, blinking in the still bright sunshine, went into the terminal. He looked around the dusty waiting area where a few Western types – cowboys and even an Indian – were hanging around, and, of course, there, wearing a delighted smile, was Patty.

She looked completely different than she did when she kissed him goodbye in New York. She had on a plaid shirt, tight jeans and a cowboy hat tilted back on her head; she had no make-up on and was lovelier than ever, twinkling eyes and that smile.

She ran up to him, squealing, "Shri Vindaloo!".

"Hey, Patty," he swept her in his arms. They stumbled against each other and ended up laughing as they always did.

"You're beautiful", he handed her the one pink rose that survived the long trip.

"You don't look so bad yourself," she smiled, kissing him gently. "Let's get out of here."

Twirling the rose in her hand, she led him to her pick-up truck. Needles was clearly a small, small, small town – there were six or seven buildings that made up the main street and, again, a dozen or so people, looking like extras in an old Western movie, going about their business quietly. Traffic was light and almost entirely made up of pick-up trucks; she gunned past them on a road clearly leading out of town.

Shri Vindaloo looked out the window at an extraordinary landscape – mostly nondescript rocks peering out of a sand bath with an occasional shrub-like tree poking up towards the sky; beyond that it looked like rolling miles of nothing. They passed no buildings and just a couple of trucks.

"What is this place? It's..it's...it's amazing!"

"Well, it ain't New York, that's for sure,"

"And it isn't Goa either. You ...you live here? But, what do you do?"

"Well, I write. I ride horses a bit, I have my dogs, Cheech and Chong," she laughed. "And it's just so amazing. I love it."

"It *is* really beautiful, in a strange sort of way. But there's nobody here – don't you get lonely sometimes."

"Well, Shri Vindaloo, I have a boyfriend." She looked at him and reached for his hand.

He was dumbfounded. He looked out the window at the desert. He didn't know what to say. His heart felt like the desert looked. She hadn't said anything about it when they met. He just thought ... and she did say she wanted him to come out and see her...

He turned to her, "Patty...?"

"I'm really sorry. I know I didn't say anything when we met – I loved meeting you and it was great on the ferry and I really wanted to see you again."

"I thought that..." he started. He took a deep breath of dry desert air, coughing. "The air is really clean," he choked.

She was looking out the windshield at the highway, out the window at the desert, anywhere but at him. "I'm sorry,

Shri Vindaloo. But I *am* glad to see you. And we can still have a good time – you'll get to see an entirely different life." She was still holding his hand.

"But, what about your boyfriend?"

"Well, he *is* crazy jealous. When I told him I had a friend I just met coming, he flipped."

"But...what...where will I stay?"

"With me, of course. He stays on the ranch, except for weekends."

"Ranch?"

"Yes, he's a cowboy."

"A cowboy? For real?"

"But, look!" The setting sun had shifted behind a huge pile of boulders and the entire horizon started to turn red. He took off his pink shades and the sky turned even redder. "That's the desert for you," she said. "Isn't it a wonder? People just don't know how many colours it has – and when it rains..."

"It rains here?" said Shri Vindaloo, confused about everything. "But, boy, its hot. I need a beer."

"Just reach in the cooler in the backseat, darlin'; and get me one while you're at it." She laughed and, for a moment, he remembered New York. "I love your pink shades."

She squeezed his hand and smiled at him. "We just need to be careful," she said as she took a swig. "I told Duane that you'd sleep in the trailer, while I'll be in the house. The trailer is a few hundred yards from the house, and, while it isn't far, at night it can be a little treacherous, particularly with the sand blowing around. But we can have a few drinks and some dinner and y'know.... We'll meet Duane tomorrow – he's got a couple of hours off and I told him we'd meet at Garcia's."

"What's Garcia's?"

"Oh, it's the local bar, the centre of town, more or less."

"Oh, OK. How far are we from your place," the sun was going down quite fast.

She had pulled off the highway into a small bumpy road. "We're almost home. Duane won't be there tonight so it'll be great. But, when we get to town, you gotta remember, you can't call me darlin', darlin'."

"Baby, this is nuts," shaking his head.

"No baby either, I'm sorry. I told you, Duane's crazy jealous."

They were bumping along and she suddenly took a sharp left and, as she pulled in, two dogs barking happily joined them. "That's Cheech and Chong, my two other darlings," she said. "Oh ...shhhheeeiit! Duane's here."

There was a beat-up old blue pickup truck parked by a pretty little wood-frame house, that, again, looked like it was lifted from the set of an old Western movie. This was where she lived – my God? And she was so New York in New York.

She jumped out of her truck slamming the door and Cheech and Chong danced wildly around her barking even more loudly. Shri Vindaloo reached for his bag from the back seat and stumbled out; he noticed she left the pink rose in the truck. She was patting, petting the dogs, "Hey, guys, this is Shri Vindaloo."

"Hey Cheech, hey Chong." The dogs turned to him, smiling; then, of course, returned to jumping at and kissing Patty.

The front door slammed opened and there was this giant – GIANT – beast in the doorway. Duane, no doubt.

"Where the fuck ya'll been," he snarled. The dogs quickly quietened down.

Patty was all over him, "Great to see you, sweetie. So nice of you to come and meet Shri Vindaloo."

She turned to Shri Vindaloo, "This is Duane, that I told you about."

He rudely pushed her aside and came down the two steps from the cabin eyeing Shri Vindaloo suspiciously.

"Hey, Duane, how's everything?" in his most cool, endearing manner, extending a manicured paw.

Towering over Shri Vindaloo, Duane enveloped his paw in an excruciating grip. "What you here for, Mister Sheree Veendaloo – what the fuck kind of name is that, anyway? How long you staying?" he growled.

"Well, I just got here and...,"

"*You cain't* stay in the house – that trailer better be good enough for you." He mercifully released Shri Vindaloo's paw and pointed at the trailer at the back of the property.

"He'll just be here a few days, Duane," Patty was now between the two of them. "I told…"

"We'll see about that," he cut her off rudely. "But I gotta leave. NOW. I'll see ya'll at Pig Dog's tomorrow at 2:30." He turned back to Shri Vindaloo. "Stay in the trailer if you know what's good for you."

He stormed off, jumped into his truck and took off in a cloud of dust and dirty exhaust.

Patty breathed a sigh of relief and the dogs got back into the we-missed-you-too act. She took off her cowboy hat. "Let's go in and get a real drink."

Shri Vindaloo was terrified. Here he was in the middle of nowhere with a crazy beast really angry with him and there was nowhere he could go. He couldn't just call a cab like he could in New York or get Eunice Pig to call him a taxi like he did in Goa.

But Patty was calming him down and, with her ministrations and a few – several – bourbons, he too began to settle in. He hadn't eaten all day, so she cooked some beans and franks and some strange desert vegetable which actually tasted amazing.

After dinner, she put together the dog's bowls and they stepped outside with their drinks.

"Look at the stars," she whispered.

He looked up and staggered, nearly falling down. There were more stars than he had ever seen – even in Goa – and they were swirling around making him dizzy. It had been a long and strange day. It was getting cold so she came closer to him and they lay together under the most romantic night with a delicate perfume and soft, sensual sighs.

Finally, she said, "I guess I should show you the trailer."

They got up, both quite drunk by this time, and, bumping into each other with Cheech and Chong trailing quietly behind, she led him into an infinite darkness. He couldn't see anything and a sandy wind whipped about his face, but she was holding his hand, leading him and, like in New York, he felt like he'd follow her anywhere. After what seemed like a long time, they reached the trailer. She pulled open the door and reaching in, took down a kerosene lamp which she lit, striking a match on her boot.

He peered in. It was small – tiny, in fact. Though it did have a bed and a sink and what looked like a toilet. She helped him into the trailer, showed him the basics and kissed him goodnight tenderly at first and then with increasing passion. But he had drunk so much that he passed out.

In the morning, he woke up not knowing where he was. Slowly, he remembered his life. He made his way to the small toilet and emptied what seemed like several gallons, and turned on the tap to wash up. He shrieked and jumped back – the water was freezing.

He pushed the trailer door open and carefully clambered down two large uneven steps and looked around.

The sun was already quite high in the sky and everything was brighter than bright. The trailer was in a sandy (of course) little clearing with some poky shrubs and a few cacti. One of the cactus plants had a brilliant pink flower. He heard a strange bird call and as he listened for more, he heard the loveliest sound he had heard in a long time

"Good morning, darlin'. Did you sleep well? It's almost eleven."

"I don't remember anything."

"Well, it was a long trip, all the way from New York," she hugged him with a sweaty kiss.

"You can say that again. And again. And again. I can't believe this place. I can't believe you live here – you seemed so at home in New York. Where do you get coffee?"

"Coming right up." They walked, still hugging, into the cabin. While it wasn't large, it was luxurious compared to the trailer and he could see it really was her home. One wall was covered with bookshelves and he saw that she had brought the pink rose from the truck and put it in a glass of water.

They had coffee and she made him some breakfast – sausages and eggs – which was delicious. He went back to the trailer and took a shower – warm, hot, steaming water – and changed into his least floral shirt. When he came out, she laughed, "You look like you're headed to Fifth Avenue. And I think you should leave the pink shades here when we go into town."

"When do we leave?"

"Well, we gotta leave," looking at her watch, "about now. I have to do some errands in town, so I'll drop you to Garcia's – you can have a beer or two – and I'll be back before 2:30, when Duane will show"

"I could go with you on the errands," nervous at being in this strange place and even stranger situation, and, of course, wanting to be with her as much as he could.

"No, that'd slow me down. People here like to talk and, of course, would be curious about you, so we'd probably be a half hour at each stop. But don't worry, Pig Dog's a real sweetheart and I'll be back before you know it."

"Who's Pig Dog?"

"Oh, Pig Dog owns Garcia's. He got that name in Nam – I guess he was something of a hero there. When he got out, he moved here and opened his place. I met him almost immediately after I got here; in fact, he helped me find the cabin – he's a really good friend. Duane knew him in Nam, and when he needed some place to settle, Pig Dog helped him get a job at the ranch."

She pulled a joint out of her top pocket, lit it and passed it to him – mmmm, good morning.

They got into the truck and headed to…God knows where. And while he had seen something of the show the evening before, the desert was even more extraordinary in the daytime, particularly after he'd had a long night's sleep. He took another drag and took off his shades. The sky was so blue it looked white; everywhere he looked there was sand, sand-coloured shrubs, sand-coloured road, sand-coloured occasional trucks passing by. He saw a ridge of mountains running to the left of them more or less in the direction they were going.

"Vegas is about four-five hours up this road."

"Whaaat? Las Vegas? But that's …that's not like this at all. I've never been there but…"

"You've never been to Vegas? You'd love it, Shri Vindaloo."

"I've seen pictures – I love all those sexy pigs dressed in feathers…"

"You would."

"Why don't we go?"

"Well, let's see – maybe we can go tomorrow. I usually go there about once a week – mostly to do laundry, though, but we could do some shows…"

"And play poker. I love to play poker – I always win. It must be my poker face."

She burst out laughing. "Poker face? You? Shri Vindaloo, you have a beautiful face, but it ain't a poker face. I think you're just a lucky pig"

"Well, I met you, didn't I?"

She had stopped the truck and was leaning across towards him. "Well here's Garcia's. Whyn't you give me a poker face kiss and I'll see you in a bit."

"Aren't you coming in?"

"Nah, like I said, I've got a lot to do – particularly if we're going into Vegas tomorrow. But Pig Dog'll know who you are – hell, by now everybody in town knows your coming. And they're all very friendly. You'll be fine."

He kissed her and jumped out of the truck – he was getting better at that too – and she was gone.

He looked around, realizing that he had, unintentionally (but sensibly) left his pink shades in the truck. But the grass was kicking in and he could still taste Patty's kiss – what the hell. He pushed open the swing doors at Garcia's feeling like a real cowboy.

It was dark inside, and, as he adjusted his eyes to the cool darkness, it seemed there was nobody there. Then, he saw this huge pig smiling at him from behind the bar.

"Hey Shri Vindaloo, welcome. I'm Pig Dog. Patty told me you were coming in and Duane said that anything you want is on his tab."

While Pig Dog was huge – bigger even than Duane – he had a gentle air about him. His grip was firm but, thankfully, not painful. Shri Vindaloo sat down on a barstool and said, "Pig Dog – what a great name!"

"It's the only one I got these days."

"Good to meet you. Can I get a beer?"

"Sure thing, and how about a shot of bourbon to welcome you properly. All on Duane, like I said."

"That's awfully nice of him."

"That's cowboy p'lite for you – you got a guest you take care of them, everything, and the best you can do, whatever else is going down. So, tell me, what brings you to these parts – I hear you're from Goa, and you met Patty in New York."

"Ah yes, Goa – that's home. And I was just in New York for a few days."

"I've heard about Goa. A couple of guys in Nam had been there and they loved it."

"Ah, Goa!" A smile spread across Shri Vindaloo's entire being. "Goa is wonderful. You must come and visit me there. The beaches are glorious, the palm trees are lovelier, the people are lovelier still, and then there's feni."

"What's feni?"

"Feni is our local drink. You drink a lot of feni and you see God. And," tapping his chest, "it puts hair on your chest."

"Sounds like a relative of tequila"

"Well, I had a tequila sunrise with Patty, which did remind me of feni. But I don't think Patty has hair on her chest."

"No, I'm sure she doesn't," with a knowing laugh. "But you know Patty's Duane's woman, right?"

"Oh yes, oh yes, of course."

"She's really something though, ain't she?" It was clear that Pig Dog had a thing for Patty, too. "Maybe I should get you a shot of tequila next. Maybe you'll see a different God."

He set up the shot with a shaker of salt and a lemon slice. Shri Vindaloo looked at the set-up, clearly confused. "Oh, that's not how your drink your – what was it – finny? Here, you sprinkle some salt on your wrist, take a lick, bite into the lemon and down the shot – if not God, you sure as hell will see something close."

Shri Vindaloo fumbled, spilling some salt and dropping the lemon, but he got the shot down. Pig Dog laughed and set up another shot, when the phone rang, and he turned to answer it.

Shri Vindaloo managed this one a little better and, looking around, saw a jukebox. He loved jukeboxes, and he had danced to so many of them with the girl pigs in New York. He dug in his pocket and fished out a dollar bill, and tried to get Pig Dog's attention.

"Your money's no good here, my friend," still on the phone. He pulled out a half a dozen quarters and pushed them over across the bar. "The best song on the jukebox is *I love my truck*."

Shri Vindaloo ambled over to the jukebox and stuck the coins in and punched in *I love my truck* and five or six others at random. What with the bourbon and the tequila and the beers and the grass and Pig Dog's graciousness, he was beginning to feel mighty fine. A song called *Mr. Bojangles* came on about a dancing pig, and Shri Vindaloo half-strutted half-jitterbugged back towards the bar.

Before he got to his stool, the swing doors slammed open and Duane and a couple of other cowboys strode in. "Hey, Sheree Veenadalo, rock 'n rolling already, huh? Pig Dog, you taking care of my friend?"

Shri Vindaloo spun around smiling, glad that he had left his pink shades behind. Duane introduced his buddies as Okie and Slim, both, again, large cowboys. They seemed very laid back and, of course, a little curious. They shook paws all around – all very civilized – and Pig Dog set them up again.

Duane picked up his shot and toasted, "To Patty's strange Goanese friend from New York," and they all downed the shots; Pig Dog, of course, set them up again. "Hey, where is she?" he asked Shri Vindaloo.

"She said she'll be here by 2:30 – another ten minutes or so, I guess."

"We're a little early, but I hope she gets here soon – I got to leave early too."

"I've heard of Goa – it's in India, right?" this from Slim, a big pig with a sweet smile.

"It is, and it's amazing," said Shri Vindaloo, warming to his favourite subject.

"They got a drink there called finny, right?" said Pig Dog. "Tastes like tequila."

"Oh, there's feni and beautiful beaches and lovely, lovely people…"

"So, what brings you to these parts then?" Slim, again.

Another round of shots showed up. It was going well – really, they seemed quite nice.

"Well, it's kind of a long story…"

"And, how do you know Patty?" still Slim.

Duane butted in. "That's what I'm here to find out."

The boys took the hint and moved across to the pool table.

Duane suddenly changed, becoming more than a little snarly. He poked Shri Vindaloo in the chest. "Look, I don't know your type. And I can't even pronounce your stupid name. But what the fuck you doing taking time off from your life and coming to see *my* woman?"

By now, Shri Vindaloo felt like they were all getting to be good friends. And so, despite Duane's aggressive tone, he smiled at him, "Hey Duane, I know Patty's your darling – she told me that last night. But," he downed the shot in front of him, "hey, man, she's not *your* woman. She's not anybody's woman, y'now. Like you can't own anyone, right?"

He immediately realized it was exactly the wrong thing to say. Duane's face started trembling like an earthquake and his eyes turned white. "What did you say, you little…"

And just at that moment, Patty walked in, "Hi darlin'"

Duane turned to the door; Shri Vindaloo did too, thanking his lucky stars.

All the boys, including Pig Dog, "Hey Patty, good to see you." You could hear the relief in their voices.

She came up to them and gave Shri Vindaloo a peck on his cheek and Duane a deep kiss. But he was incensed and shrugged her off, "I need to talk to you."

He grabbed her roughly and walked her out the door.

The bar was suddenly very quiet. Even the pool balls seemed to click more quietly. Shri Vindaloo drained his beer and ordered another.

After what seemed like a long time, Patty and Duane came back in, Duane a few steps ahead. He was still angry and stuck his fist right under Shri Vindaloo's nose, "I got to go now. But I'll be at the house tomorrow night and you better not be there!" He downed the shot that was waiting for him and headed out. "Okie, Slim, I'm gone, you coming?"

Patty, ever calm, slipped into the barstool by Shri Vindaloo who was, of course, pretty shook up. "Don't mind him," she said. "Pig Dog, get us a couple of shots, willya?"

"Sure thing, doll. We doing tequila, OK?"

"Oh sure. You know how Duane is," she said, slipping her paw onto Shri Vindaloo's lap below the bar.

"Ya, but I hadn't seen him so riled up in a long time. Shri Vindaloo, Duane's really OK, y'know, but he's got a crazy temper. He used to play pro football and had a great future with the Denver Broncos, but he couldn't keep his cool and they cut him after his first season. Which is why he had to take this shitty job at the ranch."

"Well, it'll work out. It always does." Patty downed her shot and drained her beer. "Let's get out of here, Shri Vindaloo, there's something I need to show you. Thanks forever Pig Dog."

Shri Vindaloo reached across the bar for Pig Dog's paw, "Thanks, my friend. Great place, great jukebox," he said nervously.

"Come back and see us, whenever you're this side. I'd like to hear some Goa stories."

And they were out of there. They both hopped into the truck, Shri Vindaloo, immediately putting on his shades which were on the front seat.

"So, what happened?"

"Well, y'know, we were having a drink, getting along great I thought, everyone seemed so friendly. And then, Duane said something about you being *his* woman, and I told him you can't own anyone, and he just exploded – thank God you came in when you did."

"Oh, Shri Vindaloo," she said, laughing. "You're just so silly and so open and so wonderful and definitely not a poker-faced dude, which is why I love you. But, for damn sure, it's a good thing I came in when I did. Duane has a gun and he told me he was ready to use it."

Shri Vindaloo gulped. "Well, I guess I should be making plans to get out of here."

"Ya, I think so – we'll have to do Vegas another time. But first, I got to show you something."

She turned off the road and drove further into the desert. The road turned bumpier, the shrubs got fewer and fewer, and then disappeared; there were no trees, there weren't even any boulders anywhere he looked – there was only sand, going on forever in every direction.

And, suddenly she stopped – truly, in the middle of nowhere.

"Let's get out. And leave your shades in the truck."

"We're going to meet somebody here," incredulous.

"No, no, just come with me." She had come around to his side of the truck and, grabbing his arm, pulled him out. "Let's walk for a bit."

She led him away from the truck. The sand was soft in places and filtered into his shoes – he realized why she wore boots. They tromped out further and further and, after what seemed like a lifetime, she stopped, "Look around," she said.

He did. It was completely silent and what he saw looked like nothing – everything merged into one colour, it felt like he was *inside* the horizon, there was no depth, no distance, no nothing.

"This is why I live here," she said quietly.

She held his hand and they looked around for a while – it was as if time and space had both disappeared.

Finally, she led him back towards the truck. When they got in, she said, "I love it here. It fills my soul."

Then she smiled with that twinkle back in her eye. "Let's get back to the house and have a high time tonight; I'll drop you to the bus station tomorrow."

So they did, and they did – he didn't stay in the trailer that night – and the next day, she dropped him to the bus station, complete with the pink cactus flower neatly packed in a little container to take to Goa – a remembrance of her soul and her life.

The Greatest Margarita in the World

One day, while Shri Vindaloo was walking along the beach, he came upon what looked like a very large lobster. He got closer and prodded it gently with his cane and, lo and behold, as it turned over he saw that it was actually a male porker that had clearly stayed in the sun so long that his skin had turned a bright lobster-red.

"Ah," said Shri Vindaloo, "I didn't mean to disturb you, my friend, but I think you may need something to salve your skin. My house is right over there," gesturing at a mansion nearby, "and we have some special cream that could help you."

The almost-red pig smiled through his sunglasses. "Thank you. Thank you so much, Mr. uh.."

"Shri Vindaloo is my name."

"Thank you Shri Vindaloo. I am Senor Lagarto."

"Lagarto!" cried Shri Vindaloo, surprised. "That mean's lizard in Portuguese."

"It means lizard in Spanish as well," Senor Lagarto jumped up, brushing the sand from his brightly-coloured swimsuit. Collecting his towel and manpigbag, he followed Shri Vindaloo towards the house. "Thank you so much, Shri Vindaloo, things were a bit on the boil there."

Shri Vindaloo smiled, "Lagarto is an unusual name." He remembered Galina in Leningrad, who had told him that lizards were the only creatures who had two male procreative organs. Shri Vindaloo looked discreetly towards Senor Lagarto's personal reaches but he couldn't quite tell whether things were different down there.

"I am from Mexico, Shri Vindaloo, and my family is from the area in central Mexico where they found prehistoric lizards – we were given the family name many generations ago."

A pretty little pig maiden was at the portico with two thoughtful cooling face towels. She helped Senor Lagarto to the red cement trough at the side to wash his hooves; Shri Vindaloo followed his guest and, a little cleaner and cooler, they entered the mansion. They climbed up the swirling staircase that led to the salon, which looked out over the ocean.

"Ay Caramba!" murmured Senor Lagarto. "This is grand."

"It is nice," said Shri Vindaloo happily. "Come."

He led his new friend to the easy chairs on the terrace in the shade of a small grove of joyful palm trees. The pig maiden brought two fresh coconuts with their tops sliced off neatly.

"Thank you, Sarita" said Shri Vindaloo, "and can you also bring us some caju feni and then, for Senor Lagarto, some of that special aloe vera cream that Madam Olga uses for my massage. As you see, Senor Lagarto was in the sun a little too long – he is looking almost like Senor Rosada."

"Of course, Shri Vindaloo," she smiled.

Senor Lagarto's thank yous, don't bothers ran over each other. "And what is caju feni, Shri Vindaloo."

"Feni, my friend, is the essence of Goa. It is a magical drink made from coconuts or from caju, which is cashews. Most of the time, I prefer caju feni and I think you will, too."

Sarita brought them two chilled caju fenis with a slice of lime in each, and retired shyly. Shri Vindaloo and Senor Lagarto toasted each other.

Taking a large sip, Senor Lagarto said, "Mmmm, this is fantistico – it reminds me of tequila."

Shri Vindaloo smiled broadly. "I know what you mean – I had a tequila sunrise in New York, and it did remind me a little bit of feni."

"You have been to America?"

"I was in New York recently – an amazing city!"

"That it is. But tell me, Shri Vindaloo, did you have any margaritas when you were in New York?"

"Well, I had a tequila sunrise with a beautiful lady pig who introduced me to it. And later, when I visited her in California, we had several margaritas and, of course, tequila shots, with salt and lemon."

Senor Lagarto smiled approvingly. "You do get around don't you, Shri Vindaloo?" He finished his drink and Shri Vindaloo topped up their glasses. "Well, California is closer to Mexico than New York so the margaritas must have been quite good. But," shaking his head, "the margaritas in America, particularly New York, are too... too... too sophisticated."

Shri Vindaloo nodded, "There's no end to sophistication, is there?"

"That's too true," said Senor Lagarto thoughtfully, "And so, to really taste tequila, Shri Vindaloo, you have to come to Mexico."

"I can certainly believe that. I only drink feni in Goa."

Senor Lagarto took another large swallow. "This feni really is something special – I can feel...I can feel...I don't know...I'm not drunk or anything, but I feel something else – quite ...quite..."

"That's the sunshine coming out from behind your eyes, Senor Lagarto." And sure enough, he was glowing like he was the sun itself.

Sarita came in with the body cream and, shyly signalling for Senor Lagarto to roll onto his stomach, began to gently rub the soothing cream into his glowing shoulders and back. Shri Vindaloo could tell that she was quite taken with Senor Lagarto, who was very good looking, if a bit old for her.

"Mmmm!" Senor Lagarto was enjoying Sarita's ministrations. "Shri Vindaloo, you must come visit me in Mexico. We can go in search of the greatest margarita in the world." As Sarita finished, Senor Lagarto turned around, thanking her with a kiss on the cheek. She blushed and ran inside.

Raising his glass, Shri Vindaloo said, "I have never been to Mexico. It would be a real treat, thank you."

He called out to EunicePig, who floated out to the terrace in an off-shoulder flowered caftan-of-sorts. "EunicePig, this is Senor Lagarto from Mexico."

Senor Lagarto jumped up gallantly, reaching for her paw. "Bello, senorita."

"Senora," she corrected him smiling. "But doesn't Lagarto mean lizard?"

"Yes EunicePig, Senor Lagarto is descended from a long line of lizards from ancient Mexico. And he has kindly invited me to visit him in Mexico to search for the greatest margarita in the world."

"What's a margarita?" asked EunicePig.

Senor Lagarto was still holding her paw eagerly. "It's a delicious cocktail made from tequila…"

"Which seems to be a Mexican relative of feni," said Shri Vindaloo.

"It will be marvillosa, Shri Vindaloo. And, senora, you must come too."

"Thank you, Senor Lagarto," taking her paw back, "but I won't be able to. I don't even have a passport."

"I'm sure that can be arranged..." Senor Lagarto began, but, when Shri Vindaloo signalled that he should not persist, picked up his glass. "But, at least have a feni with us. I have to leave soon and it would be such a pleasure."

"I don't drink caju feni, Senor Lagarto," she said. Again, Shri Vindaloo signalled to Senor Lagarto that he should not insist.

"Senora," still looking into her eyes, "I dream we will meet again."

"When you come downstairs, Senor Lagarto," smiling at him, "we can discuss the details for Shri Vindaloo's visit."

Senor Lagarto gulped his drink and jumped up delighted. "Thank you so much, Shri Vindaloo. I can't wait to see you in Mexico."

"Hasta la vista, my friend," surprising himself with the phrase he had learned from Patty in New York.

Shri Vindaloo settled back on his recliner, with the sun shining from behind his eyes.

After a dozy while, he suddenly heard EunicePig's mellifluous voice – she was singing.

Mama Yo Quiero,
Mama Yo Quiero,
Mammma...

He came to with a smile; it was one of the songs she used to sing quite often, before her husband, Santan, disgraced himself at the Cardinal's Christmas banquet some years ago. And even though she had, under Shri Vindaloo's coaxing, started singing again, these days she usually sang the quietly mournful fado songs. He hadn't heard her singing such a silly and joyful song in a long, long while. The glow on Shri Vindaloo's face got even brighter.

Almost an hour later, long after EunicePig had stopped singing, Senor Lagarto came out to the beach and, waving goodbye to Shri Vindaloo, wandered off towards his hotel.

Later that evening, EunicePig told Shri Vindaloo that Senor Lagarto lived in San Miguel de Allende, a city in central Mexico, and he would have to change planes in Mexico City to get there. Shri Vindaloo hummed *Mama Yo Quiero* to tease EunicePig who blushed as if she was a young senorita again.

Some weeks later, Shri Vindaloo landed, slightly jetlagged, at Mexico City International Airport. EunicePig had organized his flights so he would have a nice long layover at JFK, and, of course, had arranged for some of Shri Vindaloo's New York friends to meet him in the airline lounge. Nishisha was there, without OilyPig, who was still in Senegal; LovelyPig and PigBeauty were there, and, as a special surprise, PorkerPig, the manager from FAO Schwartz, who was working on a relationship with LovelyPig. Pigjoy was in rehearsal for a dance recital she was giving later that week, but she sent special kisses through Nishisha. They all laughed and reminisced about the Easter parade and drank a lot of champagne and several margaritas to prepare Shri Vindaloo for his mission before he boarded his flight.

An elegant senora met Shri Vindaloo at the airport in Mexico City. "I am Guadalupe, Shri Vindaloo," she said, "my baby brother, Luiz, asked me to meet you here."

"Thank you, Guadalupe," said a delighted Shri Vindaloo. She was charming and stylish and wore the most amazing bright green high heeled shoes he had ever seen. "It's such a joy to meet you."

She towered over him but took his arm quite naturally as they walked out of the airport and into the car that dropped them to the Hotel Santa Cristina. As soon as he was checked in, they went into the hotel bar.

"So, tell me about EunicePig," she said, as soon as they ordered margaritas. "Luiz can't stop talking about her. He says she sings like an angel and is even more beautiful than the Madonna."

"Ah, Guadalupe, EunicePig is amazing – more than any words could describe. And she needs someone to reopen her heart. I think your brother may be just the pig for it – I heard her sing *Mama Yo Quiero* after so many years just a few minutes after they met."

The cocktails arrived and Guadalupe toasted, "Welcome to Mexico City, Shri Vindaloo."

"Thank you, my dear Guadalupe," said Shri Vindaloo taking a healthy sip. "Mmmmm! This margarita is so much more... more...more I don't know what than the ones in New York."

Guadalupe smiled. "I think you will find that Mexico is quite as magical as Goa."

And as if on cue, the crooner, a breathtakingly lovely pig with a pout to put other lips to shame, started singing an old American jazz standard

I fall in love too easily
I fall in love too fast
I fall in love too terribly fast
For love to ever last…

Shri Vindaloo took Guadalupe's paw, kissing it as he looked into her eyes. She twinkled at him, "Shri Vindaloo, my brother told me how special you are, but…"

"There are no buts in love, Guadalupe."

"There shouldn't be, but…but I am married – happily, I must say – to Miguel, and we have two gorgeous little pigs, Delicia and Paloma."

"Congratulations!" said Shri Vindaloo raising his glass.

"Thank you, Shri Vindaloo. In another life, perhaps? But we must also have a glass of champagne to celebrate meeting." She signalled the waiter. "I have to leave soon. But, we will meet again – there's so much we have to see about – Luiz and EunicePig, for instance."

They drained their glasses and, as Shri Vindaloo rose to kiss her goodbye, their embrace was suddenly interrupted by a very excited, very young pig who rushed up and threw herself into Shri Vindaloo's arms.

There was something very familiar about her. "Shri Vindaloo!" she squealed. "How amazing to see you here. What are you doing in Mexico?"

Shri Vindaloo smiled confusedly in the double-embrace. He twisted back to finish kissing Guadalupe, but was pulled back again to the young beauty. "Shri Vindaloo, I am Ramona, Lola Flores' daughter and..."

"Ramona! My God! Look at you!" He hadn't seen her in...

"It's been nearly ten years, Shri Vindaloo."

"Let me look at you properly, my dear." He held her arms and stepped back. She was a young woman pig now but he remembered her as a little girl piglet who had worked in his house in Goa so many years ago. And he remembered how sad and happy they all were when she left to go back to her mama.

"And how is Lola Flores? And what are you doing in Mexico City? And, oh, oh, I'm sorry – this is Guadalupe, whose brother has invited me to Mexico in search of the greatest margarita in the world."

The ladies embraced, smiling. Guadalupe, who was already running late, kissed Shri Vindaloo again. "It's so nice to meet you, senorita, but I have to leave now. I'm glad that you can celebrate with Shri Vindaloo and take care of him after I leave. The hotel belongs to our family so anything you want – margaritas, champagne, food – is all taken care of."

"Ah, Guadalupe, you are as thoughtful as you are lovely. Adios – we will meet soon."

"Thank you Shri Vindaloo – you *are* as wonderful as Luiz had said. Give him my love." She looked at her watch, "I must fly."

The waiter arrived quietly with three fresh glasses of champagne and Shri Vindaloo suddenly noticed a tall young man pig standing quietly behind Ramona.

"Shri Vindaloo, this is Pedro, my friend from Cuba."

"Ah Cuba – the land of miracles! And how is Fidel?"

"You know El Comandante?" said Pedro, startled into words.

"No, but I should, shouldn't I, Ramona?"

"Of course. I'm sure he would be delighted to meet you, Shri Vindaloo – everybody is."

"But tell me, my sweet, how is Lola Flores?"

"Well, I'm sure she's great as she always is. I haven't seen her for several months – I've been at university here studying Latin music and dance."

"Like your mama."

"Shri Vindaloo, she was born doing the tango."

"Ah, Lola Flores!" with that smile on his lips.

"You should go to Buenos Aires to see her – you're so close."

"Except I have to go to San Miguel tomorrow morning. Of course, wherever whenever she summons, I will go – you know Lola Flores lights up the moon for me."

Ramona smiled, still clutching Shri Vindaloo's paw. "And this is Marta, who shares an apartment with me; Marta, this is Shri Vindaloo, who I have told you so much about." The music had stopped, and the crooner had come to their table – she was even more breathtakingly lovely up close.

"Shri Vindaloo, Ramona has told me so much about you. I have always wanted to meet you." Her lips lingered on his cheek as she sat down very close to him. The waiter had brought four margaritas and they toasted their good fortune again.

"What a great coincidence. We came in to ask Marta to go with us to Havana next week, and, in addition, we find you – such a joy."

"Love and joy are everywhere," said Shri Vindaloo.

"And silliness, Shri Vindaloo. You see, I remember."

Smiling, Shri Vindaloo blew her a kiss. "And Marta," he said, turning to her, "you sing like the moonlight. And that song – *I fall in love too easily* – was it for me?"

"Of course, Shri Vindaloo. When you came into the bar, even though I didn't know who you were, I could feel you were special and the song just came to me." He could feel her paw on his thigh.

Pedro coughed discreetly. "Uh…"

Ramona nodded at him. "We have to leave, Shri Vindaloo. Come visit us in Havana – we can dance the mambo down the Malecon, like the carnival in Goa. And go see Mama in Buenos Aires."

"Stay with me here," whispered Marta.

Shri Vindaloo rose, his head swishing from one beauty to another. He embraced Ramona, "Mi amor, you make me so proud – come back to visit us in Goa; and bring Pedro. And tell Lola Flores I await her call." They kissed on both cheeks.

"I love you Shri Vindaloo." She and Pedro kissed Marta and were gone.

When Shri Vindaloo sat back down at the banquette, he felt Marta even closer to him. Her lips up close were all he could see. And even though she wore no lipstick, his throat ran dry.

They were pulled to each other, but she stopped. "Not here, Shri Vindaloo" she whispered, "it may lead anywhere and I might lose my job."

"Let's go upstairs," started Shri Vindaloo, and they stumbled up together. Shri Vindaloo left a few ten dollar bills on the table as they hurried out.

As soon as the lift door closed, Marta kissed him, her lips devouring his. She towered over him – she also wore amazingly high heels – and Shri Vindaloo weakened into her arms till the lift stopped at his floor. They continued kissing in the corridor, stopping only for Shri Vindaloo to locate his room key and fumblingly open the door.

And as they stumbled in and onto the bed, he thought he heard a Latin version of Beethoven's Moonlight Sonata, pulsating and delicate and luscious and sweet – it carried him away.

Shri Vindaloo dozed. He had had a long series of flights and so many glasses of champagne and margaritas that he couldn't tell the difference between them.

When his eyes opened, he saw Marta, naked, perched on a chair by the window looking at him.

"Marta, you are beautiful."

She smiled and started to sing.

De la siena Morena,
Cielito Lindo,
vienen bajando...

Shri Vindaloo nearly fainted. It was so beautiful she was so beautiful he almost cried. She continued singing as she rose from the window and came to the bed. She sat by him as she came to the chorus

Ay, ay, ay, ay,
canta y no llores...,

he fell back on the pillows as she carried him to heaven.

When she finished singing, she kissed him. "I must go now, Shri Vindaloo. Its three o'clock and you have a flight in a few hours."

He couldn't even protest. He blew her a million kisses as she dressed and crept out of the room.

The next morning, Shri Vindaloo rushed to the domestic terminal for his 12:30 flight to San Miguel, which was delayed – this is Mexico, everyone said – by a couple of hours. No matter, he was still delighting in last night and yesterday and all of his life over a strong café con leche at a café/bar.

He counted as many as six brands of tequila on the shelf at the back of the bar. Hmmm...he shrugged to himself, tequila certainly isn't feni – you wouldn't find *any* brands of feni at a bar at Bombay airport, even if there was a bar at Bombay airport.

He scratched his head and looked around. The crowd was quite different from the one in the international terminal – there was more than a smattering of what looked like American pigs, but there were, of course, dozens of Mexican pigs, some with children, some with husbands and some very business-like with matching briefcases. More than a few of them wore extraordinarily high heeled shoes, like Guadalupe and Marta, and in a wide spectrum of brilliant colours. He thought of Dominic, his shoemaker in Goa, and how he could do excellent business here. Perhaps, Pig Enterprises should think about global expansion.

He boarded the short flight and, of course, Luiz was at the airport to receive him – they met as old friends, kissing each other on both cheeks, before Luiz dragged him to the airport bar for his first San Miguel margarita. "We should start with a classic tequila – Jose Cuervo."

The bartender was obviously a friend of Luiz and had been primed about their new guest. He put on quite a show and dance in mixing the cocktail and, from the first sip, Shri Vindaloo could tell that this was different even from the margaritas he had in Mexico City – it put an extra glint in his eye.

"Salud," said Luiz.

"Salud, Luiz. And to Guadalupe, your gorgeous sister – thank you for having her meet me in Mexico City. And she said you told her about EunicePig?"

Luiz was so excited. "Of course. I love Eunice Pig. Tell me about her. How is she?"

"She is a special treasure. And, of course, she said to give you her regards."

"Regards?" said Luiz, a little taken aback. "Not love?"

"Luis, she is conservative and shy. A little like me." said Shri Vindaloo, smiling.

"You're not shy, Shri Vindaloo." Luiz signalled for two more margaritas. "This time with Cuervo Lavendaro," he told the bartender. "But, tell me about EunicePig, tell me her story."

He took a sip of the next margarita. "Mmmm, this one's even better," nodding his thanks to the bartender. "EunicePig is from Santa Cruz, a village quite close to where I grew up. We would meet in church and on the promenade and here and there. She was always very special."

"Oh, yes," Luiz had a smiling look in his eye.

"And she was really a star – in school, in academics and in sports, but mostly in her singing. She sang in the choir and people came from villages far afield to listen to her at Easter."

"I can believe that – I'd come from Mexico to listen to her."

"She had suitors from all over Goa, some from very wealthy families, but she fell in love with Santan, a simple young pig from a neighbouring village. They got married and moved into a small house close to her family."

Quietly, Luiz called for another round.

"Everything seemed perfect for a few years and people began wondering when she would be expecting. But then, the mining industry in Goa closed down and Santan, who worked in the mines as a supervisor, lost his job. It was a difficult time for a lot of people in Goa. Santan, like many Goan pigs, had a taste for feni, and, unable to find work, he began to drink more and more. And more."

"Oh, dear."

"I don't know how she managed at home, but everything came out in public when, one evening at a reception at the Cardinal's house while EunicePig was singing an aria from a Konkani opera, Santan, enormously drunk and loud, made a horrible scene. I was there and what I saw..." Shri Vindaloo covered his eyes, "I can't repeat."

Shri Vindaloo took another swallow of his margarita.

"Santan disappeared and EunicePig went into hiding. Earlier, she would practice most evenings and many of us would enjoy listening to her voice when we strolled out after dinner. But after this there was a pained silence from her house. She didn't go out at all – she even stopped coming to Mass."

"Poor darling."

"I knew her – everyone knew each other in those days – and loved her from afar. So I felt I must do something. I had a saucy Goan parrot who screeched and tchtchtchtched all the time at my house. One day, I sent him over to EunicePig's house with a note asking her to teach it to sing."

He finished his cocktail and signalled no more to the eager barman.

"There was no response for what seemed like a long time and then, one day a few weeks later, I was out for the air one evening when I heard her singing with the parrot."

"Shri Vindaloo, what a beautiful story."

"What is even lovelier, Luiz, is that I have never heard her sing anything but fado – beautiful but mournful – till that day you were visiting, when she sang..."

"*Mamma yo quiero, mamma yo quiero*" Luiz sang out loud into the airport.

The waiter brought the check and Luiz escorted Shri Vindaloo out of the airport. He had a snappy red sports car in which they zoomed to the next stop (one more excellent margarita) "And now, EunicePig takes care of everything for me – she knows me better than I know myself" and the next (two more, even better) "I have to come see her again" and the next "But what about Santan?".

By this time, Shri Vindaloo was feeling a little bit drunk. "Luiz, each margarita tastes better than the last one – but might this not be the nature of the beast. Your last margarita is the best margarita?"

"But is it the greatest, Shri Vindaloo? Is it the greatest?"

"I don't know, but I'm beginning to feel a little drunk – and I haven't seen God yet."

"We have one last stop – a special one."

Shri Vindaloo noticed that they had driven into what looked like a poorer neighbourhood and everything was louder and more brightly coloured, and as they turned a corner, he saw a huge restaurant with fairy lights everywhere and huge neon signs and there was music in the streets – it was a little like Goa at Christmas.

"This is Los Consuelos, one of the oldest restaurants in San Miguel – and the best."

Luiz handed the keys to the valet, who clearly knew him well. "Buenas Noches, Senor Lagarto."

The place was jammed to overflowing but the patron, who sat at the cash register, signalled to a waiter who led them to a small table in the middle of what looked like a wild party. There was a band, playing mariachi music (Luiz told him) right by them, and there were people drinking and dancing and eating and talking very loudly. It was fantastic.

Mama Consuelo came up to them and pursing her fat lips kissed Luiz on both cheeks and hugged him close to her ample form. "Luiz, Luiz, Luiz – demasiado tiempo – este es tu amigo?" and enveloped Shri Vindaloo is her joyous embrace. She shouted over the mariachis, "Margarita, margarita!"

"No, no, Mama Consuelo," Luiz pulled her to him and whispered something in her ear.

"Ay caramba! Fantastico!"

She disappeared briefly and returned with a cloudy-looking bottle, wiping it with a dirty cloth. "Mescal!" she shouted triumphantly.

Luiz explained to Shri Vindaloo that mescal is the magic root of tequila and the secret of real mescal is that it has a worm in the bottle. "I swallowed the worm once – it was terrible, but" unbuttoning his shirt, "it grows hair on your chest."

Mama Consuelo held the bottle up before Shri Vindaloo. "Porko Grande," she said, "you must eat worm…" biting her teeth, "like this." And she laughed excitedly.

Shri Vindaloo jumped onto the table as Mama Consuelo poured him a large shot with a wriggling worm trying to climb out of the shot glass. Shri Vindaloo tried to grasp the slippery devil, and with a crowd around them egging him on, he caught it between two fingers and, as it danced in the air, took a bite. The crowd roared.

It was delicious. "Deliciosa," he said, and, popping the smaller bit of the still-wriggling worm into his mouth, chased it with the shot. Mama Consuelo climbed on the table too and poured him another shot. It was amazing – he could feel more hair growing on his chest. This was a rough and ready relative of caju feni.

The mariachi band was suddenly playing Cielito Lindo and Shri Vindaloo remembered Marta – was it only last night – but as Mama Consuelo sang *Ay, ay, ay, ay,* he had to join her. She had a deep voice and while she sang words in Spanish, he sang along "*La la la la la, la la la la la la,*" till she came back to the chorus and the whole restaurant, it seemed, sang along.

There was more mescal and more beer and more music and more dancing and more food and Shri Vindaloo ended up being carried around the restaurant like King Momo at the Goa carnival. It was a great night and at some point in the wee hours, the patron arranged for someone to drive them to Luiz' apartment.

The next morning, which was really the next afternoon, they rose to a lovely breakfast – coffee, of course, and papaya juice, tortillas and beans and eggs and the most scrumptious cornbread in the world – served on the terrace by an elderly slow-moving pig.

"Thank you, Viernes," said Luiz and, sounding not fully revived, "It was quite a night. I have never seen Mama Consuelo the way she was with you last night."

"She was amazing, and my head is still throbbing after all that mescal and...."

"And that heart-stopping story you told me about Eunicepig. I must come back to see her...but..."

"There are no buts in love, Luiz, as I told Guadalupe."

"But this is different – I love EunicePig but it is ... it is ... very difficult because of my family curse."

"What family curse, Luiz?"

Luiz was a bit uncomfortable. "Shri Vindaloo, I feel we are more than brothers so I can tell you the truth. My family has a long history and, as I told you, is descended from the pre-historic lizards that used to roam this area of Mexico. And, while the curse is thinning out, some of the males in my family are born, like lizards, with two penises!'

"Ay Caramba!" said Shri Vindaloo, beginning to feel a little bit Mexican. He thought again about Galina and shot a quick discreet glance at Luiz' pyjama bottoms. "I wondered about the name Lagarto."

"My great-grandfather had the curse. And, after him, me," said Luiz disconsolate.

"But, this should be a blessing, no?" His mind was boggling.

"Well," said Luiz smiling mischievously, "Some American pigs seem to like it, which is why I go so often to Americano, the first bar we stopped at." Shri Vindaloo remembered Luiz being eagerly greeted by several white lady pigs. "But, I have had some Mexican senoritas run screaming from my bed, and, now, none of the good Mexican families will allow their young girl pigs near me. So, I am all alone and sad."

"But Luiz, I, too, am all alone – and I am never sad."

"Shri Vindaloo, you are different – everyone loves you as soon as they meet you. But I, Shri Vindaloo, ...I want to be married and have a family. And EunicePig..." he smiled shyly.

"Ah, EunicePig," Shri Vindaloo smiled back at him. "Luiz, I didn't tell you this, but right after you left my house, I teased her about you and she blushed like a virgin pig. Come back to Goa and, perhaps, EunicePig will see your family curse as a blessing."

"But is she still married to Santan? And where is he?"

"Nobody knows, but some people say he has moved to England. But Luiz, don't worry – EunicePig is more modern than me or even you, so..."

Luiz brightened and walked pensively out to the terrace.

"It's a glorious day, Shri Vindaloo – let's go to the market."

After a slowly luxurious toilet, the caballeros climbed into Luiz' sports car and sped off. The market was about twenty minutes away and it took some time for Luiz to find a parking spot. Shri Vindaloo gazed, a little glassy-eyed, at the vibrant colours everywhere with stalls that sold everything from food to drinks to clothes to household wares to toys to little this-and-thats to – Ay caramba! Sombreros!

There were wide brims and wider brims, there were sombreros with little charms hanging from the brims, small sombreros with little animals woven into the straw, sombreros with pretty ribbons and...wa-ayy at the back of the stall, a pink sombrero.

Shri Vindaloo tried it on and, of course, it fit perfectly.

"Shri Vindaloo, you look like a Mexicali Rose – male version, of course," said Luiz, laughing out loud.

Shri Vindaloo strutted down the market road, smiling at his delighted audience, who cheered him with many "Buenos Dias"es. As they came to the end of the main drag of the market, he saw a bar with Western swing doors and a broken-down sign saying Tio Sam's.

Luiz tried to wave him away. "That's not the kind of place we should go into, Shri Vindaloo – certainly not the way I feel right now. And, in any case, we wouldn't get margaritas there."

"What does Tio mean?"

"Tio means 'uncle'"

"Uncle Sam's! We must go in, Luiz – I love America!"

And before Luiz could protest any more, Shri Vindaloo, in his pink sombrero, had swung open the barroom doors announcing himself loudly. The bar was a small, damp, dark room with a half dozen or so groggy customers sitting at tables around the room. A few of them looked up and grunted – the pink sombrero, no doubt – but no cheery Buenos Dias.

Near the door, two pigs had their heads down on a table as if they were asleep or passed out or something; from their dress and demeanour, he couldn't tell whether they were male or female or what. The whole room smelled of stale cigarette smoke and spilled beer – it looked like it had been a rough Saturday night.

Luiz had walked in by then. He wrinkled his nose and, taking Shri Vindaloo by the arm, escorted him to an adjacent room. There were two pigs stretched out on the floor, one on his back and the other on his stomach; the room smelled even worse. "Let's get out of here," said Luiz.

"No, no," said Shri Vindaloo. "Let's at least get a beer – this is Uncle Sam's, after all."

He bellied up to the bar and, smiling in his usual winning way, he held up two fingers, "Cerveza, please."

The bartender, who was of a grizzled piece with his customers, cracked open two longnecks. Shri Vindaloo laid a couple of dollar bills on the bar and handed one of the beers to Luiz. He took a swig of his beer and swanned over to the jukebox.

"I love jukeboxes," he said to the room – Luiz was wanting to get out and nobody else was listening. Shri Vindaloo mouthed the names of the songs, all in Spanish, of course. Some of them sounded vaguely familiar, and then... "Aha!" he almost shouted. "Cielito Lindo."

He punched the numbers in and, even before the song started up, Shri Vindaloo sang, "*La la, la la la, la la, la la la…*"

There was a stirring in the room. And by the time he came to the chorus, *Ay, ay, ay, ay*, which he sang lustily, one of the sleeping/passed out pigs raised his/her head and, looking straight at Shri Vindaloo, said, in a demanding voice, "I laaav you."

Shri Vindaloo turned to the pig, smiling. By now, he was swaying to the music, dancing around the bar and singing. At the next chorus, the pig rose from the table – she was a strangely beautiful, if extraordinarily unkempt, pig. "I laaaaav you," she insisted.

She staggered her way up to him, and whispering, "Venga conmigo", dragged him out of the bar.

Luiz called out, "Wait!" and rushed to the door.

He saw Shri Vindaloo in her deep embrace, his pink sombrero already on her head.

"Shri Vindaloo!" he called out. "Where are you going?"

Shri Vindaloo turned back, smiling, "Luiz – this is Margarita."

She waved and they were gone towards the *barrio*.

A few days later, Shri Vindaloo showed up at Casa Lagarto with an intoxicated smile in his eyes.

"Shri Vindaloo, where have you been? I was so worried – I looked and looked in the *barrio* but nobody knew where you were."

But seeing his smile, Luiz smiled as well. "So I called EunicePig to tell her you were lost and she told me not to worry." He was quite excited. "And she sang to me and we had a long delicious chat."

"You see, Luiz, it always works out."

"You're right, Shri Vindaloo, as always. And we have made plans for me to come back to Goa."

"That's wonderful." Shri Vindaloo said. "And now I, too, can now return to Goa since our assignment is complete – as you saw, I found the greatest Margarita in the world."

He smiled, bowed and went to bed.

Laissez Les Bon Temps Rouler

S hri Vindaloo snapped out of his nap as the plane hit the tarmac. He blinked awake thinking, are we here already? The flight coming into Mexico had seemed much longer, but then that also seemed like several lifetimes ago.

The plane taxied towards the terminal and, as it came into view, he read LOUIS ARMSTRONG INTERNATIONAL AIRPORT. The pilot announced, "Welcome to N'awlins, the home of jazz, great food and wonderful cocktails."

Shri Vindaloo looked around confused. He thought he was going to New York *en route* to Goa. He remembered that he had been awakened very, very early that morning by a hysterically happy Luiz. "Shri Vindaloo, wake up, wake up. WAKE UP. I called EunicePig and asked her to marry me."

Shri Vindaloo rubbed his eyes. "Ahhhh!" he smiled.

"And," said Luiz, even more excited, "she said yes! Not just yes, she said, YES, OF COURSE!"

Shri Vindaloo sat up in bed. "My dear Luiz. Congratulations!" And he blew him a two-pawed kiss.

"But..." Luiz was, as often, uncertain.

"Luiz, there are no buts in love."

"But...but...well, I guess that's true, but, but EunicePig said that she was still married to Santan. So how can we get married?" His words were stumbling over one another. "But she also said that the Pope is coming to Goa in a few months and you will be able to convince him to give us a special dispensation." In amazement, "You know the Holy Father, Shri Vindaloo?"

"Il Popa? No, I've never had the pleasure. Don't worry, Luiz, I'm sure EunicePig will speak to the Cardinal and arrange something."

"And she also asked when you would be returning – she misses you."

"I miss her, too, particularly with this joyous news. And, since our assignment is complete, I am ready to go back."

"I know," said Luiz. "I've arranged for both of us to fly to Mexico City this afternoon – Guadalupe is waiting to see you – and then you can carry on home."

"Oh, thank you Luiz. I can't wait to meet Guadalupe again."

"And she has something she wants you to take to EunicePig."

After a delicious breakfast of avocados and coffee and avocados and tortillas and avocados and avocados, they headed to the airport, and in a couple of hours were embracing Guadalupe in Mexico City. This time her shoes were even more brilliant, a dramatic mix of midnight blue and turquoise, and the heels were, if anything, even higher. She took them both, one by each arm and walked them to the Mi Corazon bar.

"What a perfect place to talk about love," she said, smiling at her brother. "Shri Vindaloo, thank you for taking care of my brother's heart – Luiz told me that EunicePig has said yes."

Luiz had a foolish, besotted smile on this face.

"Love is all there is, Guadalupe. Speaking of which, how is Miguel? And Delicia and Paloma?"

"They are so delightful – I told them about you and they can't wait to meet you."

"It won't be long now," Shri Vindaloo smiled into her eyes.

"We must toast our new family bond," said Luiz. "But only champagne – no more margaritas. Shri Vindaloo already found the greatest margarita in the world."

Guadalupe smiled knowingly, and looked around as three glasses of champagne appeared. "And I have a gift for EunicePig." She took a jewellery box from her handbag, and, snapping it open, she handed it to Shri Vindaloo.

It was a pair of earrings of exquisitely brilliant yellow stones set in silver. "Caramba!" he marvelled, "I've never seen stones this colour." Sniffing them, "They even smell of Mexico."

"They *are* very special and are only found in our part of Mexico. They are called *ojos de lagarto* – lizard's eyes."

"EunicePig will faint with delight," said Shri Vindaloo.

"These earrings belonged to our great-grandmother," said Luiz. "You remember, Shri Vindaloo, I told you that my great grandfather was the last male in our family to have the curse…"

"But didn't you always say that it was a blessing, Luiz?" teased Guadalupe. "With the American girls?

Luiz shushed her, blushing. "Shri Vindaloo, we want EunicePig to have these for her … for our … family's protection."

"Luiz, Guadalupe – you are both so thoughtful and caring. And," holding them up to the light, "the earrings are beyond beautiful. I will give them to EunicePig with your love."

Luiz was still nervous and, of course, excited. Guadalupe took his paw, "Remember, Luiz, our grandfather, his two brothers and all of their male children were not affected by whatever it was, blessing or curse."

"Luiz," Shri Vindaloo embraced him. "EunicePig already knows you are a unique blessing."

In all this, the flight was called, they downed their champagne and Shri Vindaloo grabbed his passport and boarding card from the table and skipped towards the gate, with brother and sister waving and smiling in a joyful embrace.

I must have picked up the wrong boarding pass, he thought, smiling and thanking the pretty stewardesses as he deplaned.

He stepped into the terminal and was greeted by a giant fluorescent green lizard. My God, lizards are everywhere. He looked more closely and saw that the lizard was actually a swimming float and a smiling, handsome face peered out from behind it.

Shri Vindaloo smiled back. "Buenos Dias, senor, are you from Mexico?"

"Mexico? No," said the pig, coming out fully from the float and looking eagerly behind and around Shri Vindaloo. He seemed to be expecting someone.

"I've just come from Mexico – the land of lizards," said Shri Vindaloo, holding out his paw.

"Mexico? I thought this was the flight from Houston."

He rushed towards the adjoining gate, dragging the bright green lizard and still holding Shri Vindaloo's paw. "Oh, good, the Houston flight still hasn't landed." He slowed down and focused on his new friend. "Are you from Mexico?"

"No, no, I am Shri Vindaloo from Goa."

"Goa? Isn't that in India? I've always wanted to go to India."

"Ah, you must come visit me in Goa, Mr. uh…"

"My name is Zacharay Francisco Richard, but you can just call me Zack. And you…"

"Shri Vindaloo."

"That's a strange name. How do you pronounce your name?"

"It's quite simple, Zack," said Shri Vindaloo, preening a bit. "It's like 'she' with an 'r'"

"Oh, Shree, that's simple."

"No, not Shreeeee, Zack, you can clip it off to 'Shri'."

"Oh, OK, Shri Vin-daloo – very good. So, Shri Vindaloo, what took you to Mexico?"

"I went to visit my friend Luiz to find the greatest margarita in the world."

"Ooooh," Zack licked his lips. "I've had a lot of delicious margaritas – that sounds like quite an adventure."

"It certainly was, and we did."

"Did?"

"We found it – the greatest margarita in the world."

"You did? Where? What was it like?"

"In a small bar in San Miguel, and it wasn't an 'it', it was a 'she'."

"Not a shree, huh?" laughed Zack.

"No, no, no." Shri Vindaloo smiled, this Zack is funny. "No, we drank a lot of margaritas in different bars, but the best – by many, many miles – turned out to be this grizzled but lovely lady pig whose name was Margarita. I had played Cielito Lindo on the jukebox and I wasn't even thinking of margaritas and she came up and grabbed me."

"Wow, Shri Vindaloo!" He dropped the lizard float and applauded. Zack looked around as he picked it up, "So, where is she?"

Shri Vindaloo looked around as well. "She's still in San Miguel in the *barrio*. When we met, or when she took charge of me, I didn't know she was married. After a couple of days, her husband showed up so I had to leave suddenly in a hurry. But, in any case, I have to go back to Goa urgently to organize Luiz' wedding with EunicePig and, instead, here I am in New Orleans."

"Whoa, whoa – Luiz, EunicePig, wedding? That's a lot of life, but life is never urgent, Shri Vindaloo. Pearlie is coming in from Houston and we're going to the zydeco festival in Abbeville in the bayou – you must join us."

"What's zydeco? Is it like tequila?"

Zack laughed. "No, no, my friend," and laughed and laughed. "Zydeco is not a drink; it's music from around here, Cajun country, which spreads from the bayou – the Mississippi delta – up through New Orleans and even east of here," still laughing, "But," thinking aloud, "y'know you may have something there – dancing to zydeco does sometimes feel like drinking a lot of tequila."

The Houston flight had landed by this time and a big blond pig came running out of the aerobridge and threw herself onto Zack and the giant green lizard. "Za-a-aaaa-ack," she screeched, as they fell to the floor.

"Pearlie, my Cajun darlin'," as he extricated himself from her lipsticked embrace. "You just so bright and so wild. And so tasty," smacking his lips. "I want you to meet my new friend Shri Vindaloo – he's from India and just landed here from Mexico."

"Ah, Me-hico," Pearlie smiled blowing Shri Vindaloo a pouty kiss.

"He's coming to Abbeville with us. He's never even heard of zydeco – he thought it was a drink like tequila!" And they all laughed. "Shri Vindaloo just found the greatest margarita in the world in Mexico, so dancing to zydeco is the natural next step and I have some Thai stick that will help us really take off."

Zack ran off to get the car and Shri Vindaloo held on to the green lizard float while Pearlie lit a cigarette. She was a large pig in bright, tight capri pants and a tight green T-shirt, which said – again? – Lizardland Texas. And, seemingly out of character, she wore a double string of pearls around her neck.

"I love your pearls, Pearlie" said Shri Vindaloo.

"I always wear them." She smiled a sweet acknowledgement.

"And I really love your lipstick."

Her smile got broader.

"You know the second best place for a pig lady's lipstick, don't you Pearlie?" Shri Vindaloo reached his head forward, snout pursed.

Pearlie burst into laughter and, reaching across the float, planted a soft one on his lips.

A light green convertible screeched to a stop. Zack pulled a plastic baggie from the lining of his cap and tossed it to Pearlie. "Pearlie, you get in the back and roll us a few; Shri Vindaloo, you jump in front with me – you can give the alligator to Pearlie."

They pulled out of the parking garage onto the crowded freeway and before they had gone even half a mile, Pearlie put both arms around Zack's neck and stuck a big fat joint into his mouth. He took a deep drag, "Ah, Coca cola," he sang, passing the joint over to Shri Vindaloo. He pushed the button on the radio and a foot-stomping rhythm blasted from it with all three of them instantly head-shaking in time.

Shri Vindaloo had never heard music like that before – he had danced non-stop during the carnival in Goa, and, of course, the mariachi music with Mama Consuelo, but this was more... more...more and then suddenly sweetly romantic. Pearlie, who had the joint, screamed, "That's Clifton Chenier, my granddaddy! Laissez les bon temps rouler!"

She was dancing from side to side in the back seat, leaning over and kissing Zack on the neck, passing the joint to Shri Vindaloo, taking it from him, kissing his neck, passing the joint over to Zack and on and on.

"That's zydeco, Shri Vindaloo" said Zack. "Let the good times roll!"

He suddenly slammed on the brakes, stopping the car in the middle of the road, and jumped out. Pearlie, nimble beyond her size, leapt from the back seat and pulled Shri Vindaloo out as well. They danced on the highway till the song and the next one and the next one ended, and then, hugging and kissing each other, jumped back in and got on the road again.

Pearlie found some beers in a cooler in the back seat, which she passed around, and rolled another joint and with zydeco full blast the trip to Abbeville seemed to take no time at all, so much so that they barely noticed a brief thunderstorm that soaked them to their skins.

The festival was – my god, the zydeco festival! Live music, louder and wilder than on the radio, hundreds of multi-shaped and multi-coloured pigs singing and shouting and drinking and dancing and... y'know...the good times were rolling. Zack and Pearlie and Shri Vindaloo danced and staggered around and drank more beers and smoked more marijuana and ate red beans and rice and crawfish etouffee, and were having more than a good ol' time.

After some time, Pearlie and Zack slipped away for some – uh – privacy, and Shri Vindaloo wandered around on his own, browsing through the stalls, some selling food and drink and some with clothes and some with hand-made artefacts and other trinkets.

At one of the stalls, a tall pig with a huge mane of long, stringy hair, hailed him, "Hey Mister, where you from."

"I'm from Goa, in India," said Shri Vindaloo, smiling back.

"India! Wow, maaan – I lu-u-v India. Come and look at this."

Shri Vindaloo, who was still dragging the bright green float around, went into the stall where the man showed him a small ivory Buddha; it had a silver chain through its head so you could wear it around your neck.

"Ah, the perfect master!"

"No-o-oh maaan, *this* is the *Imperfect* Master," he smiled, showing very large and slightly dirty teeth. "I got him in India last year and cleaned out his brains, so I could run the chain through. So, now he is perfectly imperfect, like all of us."

"Perfectly imperfect?" said Shri Vindaloo amazed. "How fantastic!"

"Yeah maaan. You know, the brain is like a toothbrush – good for brushing your teeth," showing his molars again, "but you cain't use it for much else. The brain's like that – it works for a few things but you sure as hell cain't use it for living your life, maaaan. That's why the Imperfect Master has his brain cleaned out."

"How perfect – or, maybe I should say, perfectly imperfect. Can I buy this – it's perfect for a friend of mine."

"Welcome to Abbeville," said our spiritually-evolved merchant. He wrapped the little treasure in a delicious piece of bright pink tissue paper and namaste'd Shri Vindaloo who thanked him and wandered off.

He bought a beer and, still trailing the float, came upon a small lake where a group of Cajun pigs were partying. Some of the girl pigs, many of whom, like Pearlie, were quite large, had jumped in and out of the lake and were showing off all their glorious parts. One of the male pigs, Beau, had taken off most of his clothes and ran into the water signalling Shri Vindaloo to follow. Shri Vindaloo was dancing with Cam-mie, one of the Cajun girl pigs and as they danced down towards the water, Beau came up for air with a small glass bottle, which he unscrewed and stuck under Shri Vindaloo's snout.

Shri Vindaloo felt his heart begin to pound. He looked around at Cam-mie, but she was dancing in her own dream. And then, suddenly, he found himself laughing and laughing like a fool. Beau said conspiratorially, "That's amyl nitrate – they use it in hospitals to get dying peoples' hearts going again." And he laughed and cackled and laughed and laughed. He took another snort and passed the bottle to Shri Vindaloo, who sniffed again and, after a few seconds, started laughing again. Camille came running over, "I want some." She kissed Shri Vindaloo and took a sniff of the bottle and they burst out laughing together, and fell to the ground kissing and laughing. They clambered onto the float and lay in each other's arms, laughing and kissing and being silly. Laissez le bon temps rouler, hollered Cam-mie.

After a while, Pearlie and Zack came back and Pearlie called out, "Hey, darlin', we gotta go."

Shri Vindaloo kissed Cam-mie till they fell back into the lake laughing. He climbed out, blew her another kiss and bye-byed his new friends.

They had a hell of a time finding the car but they did. And Zack, smoking another joint, pulled out of the jammed parking area. Pearlie was in the front seat now and had the radio tuned to a classical station while Shri Vindaloo dozed like the dead.

When he woke up, he was laying fully-clothed but with his shoes off on the bedspread in a room with bright sunshine streaming in the windows. He had no idea where he was but staring straight at him was a smiling pink elephant with purple spots running across the wall with three odd birds and several stars following him. He gave them all an early morning smile.

He went downstairs and found Zack and Pearlie drinking coffee in the kitchen. "Shri Vindaloo!" they said together, "it's way past noon. I guess you slept well."

"Like a baby, with zydeco dreams," he said, "and you were both in it – what a party!"

"Welcome to New Orleans," said Zack.

"And I love the mural in the bedroom. It makes me think of a magic circus." He looked around and saw that the kitchen wall had more strange birds, palm trees and – of course – an alligator, all in the same wondrous unfinished style.

"Work in progress, Shri Vindaloo," said Zack modestly.

"You need some coffee?" said Pearlie, getting up for a refill.

"Yes please, it smells mmm mmm mmm…"

She poured him a mug and Shri Vindaloo took a big swallow. "My God, this is amazing – I've never tasted coffee like this."

"It's a blend of chicory and coffee," Pearlie smiled and air-smooched him. "We Cajuns have this running through our veins."

Shri Vindaloo took another long swallow. "Zydeco, chicory coffee – what else you got?"

"We just getting started, Shri Vindaloo. We can go down to the Quarter and start with brunch, have a couple of beers, wander around outside – there's always music somewhere, maybe we could go to Tipitina's later…"

"Yaah," Pearlie broke in, "Maybe Professor Longhair will be playing."

"It all sounds fantastic," Shri Vindaloo refilled his coffee mug. "And I need to figure out getting back to Goa – not urgent, nothing's urgent, like you said, Zack."

"Well, let's start at Napoleon House – it's the best place to take care of business."

Slow slow quick quick foxtrot shower and change at the end of which they looked like the better part of fifty million dollars with Pearlie, who had put on a large straw hat, carrying the biggest share. They stepped out and was it hot! Hot. Hot. Hot. Really hot.

"This is hotter than Goa."

"We like it this way, Shri Vindaloo. C'mon here's a cab."

All three of them piled into the back seat and as the cabdriver took off, Zack turned to Shri Vindaloo, who was at the other window, with Pearlie, who had rolled another joint, a wonderful squeeze between them. "Shri Vindaloo, this is Saint Charles Avenue, the grandest avenue in the world."

Shri Vindaloo was torn between looking at the old mansions on both sides of the beautiful tree-lined avenue, enjoying Pearlie's squeeze, and taking the joint. "And why don't you tell Pearlie about the greatest margarita in the world?"

With several "look how lovely's" out the window, it took some time to tell the tale and Pearlie whooped when he told the part about Margarita, "Shri Vindaloo, you always get the girl don'tcha?" She reached over and kissed him.

By this time the cab had pulled into the French Quarter and Shri Vindaloo was even more wowed. "My God! This is amazing – look at the wrought iron railings on the balconies; it reminds me of Fontainhas. And look at that wild pig on the cycle." An elderly pig in pink pants and what looked like a hat made from pantyhose almost rammed into the cab and cyclestaggered off.

"Welcome to the French Quarter, Shri Vindaloo," said Zack, "and here we are at Napoleon House."

He settled the cab and they trooped in to the darkly-daylit bar. Pearlie led the way to the private table in the corner just by the phone booth. As if it were waiting for them, the phone rang. Zack picked it up and got into an animated conversation.

"This is Zack's office," said Pearlie, as she and Shri Vindaloo sat down and she called out for three Dixie beers.

"What a special place to do business," said Shri Vindaloo. "And what is his business?

"Lots of things. He paints, as you've seen, and he buys and sells stuff," pointing to the phone, "but mostly he just has a good time. That's why I love him. And what about you, Shri Vindaloo? What is your business?"

"Well," said Shri Vindaloo, picking up one of the beers, "lots of things, like you said. My company, Pig Enterprises, has coconut plantations, that were in the family for a long time, and now we also do research on coconuts and sunshine and happiness, and…."

"Happiness!" Pearlie picked up her beer. "I'll drink to that. And how's business?"

"Oh, business is good, it's very good. You know, to run a business you need to have some skills – like you and Zack both have – and you have to work hard – maybe – and, of course, you have to be lucky. And," smiling at her through his beer, "I'll take luck over brains any time."

"I'll drink to that, too."

Zack came off the phone and sat down smiling.

"And to be happy," pointing at Zack, "all you have to do is smile."

Suddenly remembering, he pulled the crumpled pink tissue from his pocket and clasped the Imperfect Master around Zack's neck. "This reminded me of you, Zack."

Pearlie reached across Shri Vindaloo almost climbing onto his lap to inspect the little medallion. "It's so cute – it looks like a Buddha."

"Well, it *is* the Buddha but he's had his brains cleaned out. The man in Abbeville said the Buddha with his brains cleaned out is the Imperfect Master, which makes him perfectly imperfect, like all of us."

"How perfect," said Pearlie.

"Thank you so much, Shri Vindaloo." Zack kissed Shri Vindaloo on both cheeks and Pearlie a hot one on the lips. "I guess I always had a sense of it, but now I know I'm perfectly imperfect. How fabulous!"

"How perfect," said Pearlie.

"And now, how about some breakfast?"

"I want scrambled eggs and oysters," said Pearlie, licking her lips. "And what about you, Shri Vindaloo, father of the Imperfect Master."

"Scrambled eggs and oysters sound amazing."

An old, little stooped-over and smiling waiter came over, took their orders and shuffled off.

"So, Shri Vindaloo, now tell us about this wedding."

Pearlie called out for more beers and Shri Vindaloo told them the story about meeting Luiz near his house in Goa and how he introduced him to EunicePig and how they fell in love and – leaving out the lizard parts story – how Luiz proposed to her and how she said yes, of course.

"The most amazing thing is that they've never even kissed – and, here they are, getting married!"

"That's as pure as love can be," sighed Pearlie, looking lovingly at Zack.

"And love is all there is," said Shri Vindaloo nodding.

The scrambled eggs with oysters, red beans on the side and some French bread arrived. Pearlie immediately tore off a few pieces and passed them around. Shri Vindaloo buttered his bit up and popped in his mouth, and stopped, amazed, mid-bite. "This is just like toasted poi."

"What's poi?"

"It's the bread I have every day for breakfast in Goa – this feels more and more like home."

"Welcome to New Orleans, yet again."

"So I need to talk to EunicePig."

"We could call her right now," said Zack going to the phone booth.

"Isn't there a time difference?" this from Pearlie.

"Love doesn't know about time or time differences," said Shri Vindaloo, taking the phone from Zack. "EunicePig, congratulations! – Luiz told me you said, yes of course."

"Shri Vindaloo, how great to hear your voice. Where are you?"

"I'm in a phone booth in New Orleans with Zack and Pearlie."

"New Orleans? Who are Zack and Pearlie?"

"Some wonderful pigs I met at the New Orleans airport."

"Why'd you go to New Orleans?"

"It's a long story, my dear, as always. New Orleans is an amazing place. We – you, Luiz and I – must come here."

"Of course. But when are you coming back? I miss you."

"I leave tomorrow and will be back in Goa by early the day after."

"Oh, good," said EunicePig, "I can't wait to see you." Her voice dropped a little. "But, Shri Vindaloo, Santan has come back."

"Whaaat? When?" Shri Vindaloo wasn't easily shocked.

"You know his mother and mine are old friends and Auntie Piedade came over and told my mum that Santan has come back and…"

"Don't say anything to Luiz yet, EunicePig," said Shri Vindaloo in a hurry. He knew his friend would tear his hair out with worry.

"No, no, no, I haven't," said EunicePig. "He calls me twice a day – he is so sweet and lovely." He could see her smile.

"Don't worry darling. We'll figure it out."

"As long as you're around, Shri Vindaloo I'm never worried."

He kissed her loudly through the phone and hung up.

Zack had settled the bill and called the waiter back. "Let's get some Old Fashioneds to go and show Shri Vindaloo the Quarter."

They stepped out with their drinks and Shri Vindaloo's head and eyes rolled around and around again. Pearlie had rolled another joint which they were passing around discreetly. Delighted after speaking with EunicePig, Shri Vindaloo felt like hugging everyone he passed. Some were wild and fabulous girl pigs and some were strange scraggly pigs – kind of like Margarita – where you couldn't tell whether they were this way or that. Some of them had silly hats on their heads, some wore rows and rows of beads, some were bare-chested – it looked like it a party.

"It's always like this in the quarter," said Zack.

Pearlie was leading the way swinging her hips dancing to the music of the city. An old and decrepit pig with a brightly-coloured cocktail glass came up and joined her for a bit, but when he got too close, she just cackled and popped him gently on the head with her straw hat and moved on.

"Ain't she something?" smiled Zack, as he pulled her back for a kiss.

They wandered by an antique store and Shri Vindaloo suddenly heard a brilliant yellow feather boa calling to him from the shop window – it was just the colour of EunicePig's new earrings. How perfect. He went in to buy it and found several others; one was an almost-vibrating emerald green – it was obviously for Pearlie. She had followed him in and he draped it across her upswept shoulders, making her look as funky regal as she truly was. As she preened and pouted and flounced around the store, she saw a luscious lipstick pink boa; she grabbed it and, brushing Shri Vindaloo's lips with a smile, spread it as it belonged across his shoulders.

And as they laughed and camped it up in front of the mirror, he saw reflected deep in the dusty back of the store, another feather boa, this one a deep midnight blue with turquoise highlights. "Guadalupe," he said triumphantly.

Pearlie started. "Who's Guadalupe?"

"Ah, Guadalupe," sighed Shri Vindaloo. "So stylish, so sophisticated, so sexy, and just ... just so... so perfect. No," he said hurriedly. "Perfectly imperfect."

"Shri Vindaloo, you sound smitten. Where is she? We must meet her."

"She's in Mexico City. She's Luiz' sister. And she's married and has two little pigs." With his usual happy smile, "And she will always be special to me."

"Tell me more," Pearlie was pulling at his arm.

"I've said all I will," smiled the pig patriarch, kissing her cheek gently. "You'll meet her at the wedding."

Shri Vindaloo paid for the boas and they went back outside, Pearlie and Shri Vindaloo, by now quite the French Quarter aficionados with the brilliant boas across their shoulders around their necks and their squealing heads high in the air.

Zack had dipped into another bar and come out with three more to-go drinks. "Professor Longhair ain't in town," he said, "but I just heard about this wild blues bar over on Magazine street down by the projects – we should go there later."

It was way past dusk but still hot and the craziness and the music and the loud crowds got even crazier and louder as they got to Bourbon Street. Shri Vindaloo, friendly as always, stopped to chitchat with every passing stranger, particularly the groups of college girl pigs who loved his pink boa; the college boys and wayward drunks had eyes only for Pearlie. They tapdanced with the little black pigs in the street and would have still been there if Zack hadn't pulled them away towards Preservation Hall, singing *"Oh, I went down to Saint James Infirmary..."*

The show was almost over but Zack knew the guy at the door who let them into the packed room which was rocking to the rafters. And when the band burst into "The Saints", it felt like the roof would blow off.

They left as the show ended and wandered in and out of a few more bars, getting bourbon shots here, a couple of Old Fashioneds there, a beer every now and then, till Zack hailed a passing cab and they all jumped into the back seat, Pearlie already rolling another joint.

"We're going to that old blues bar on Magazine near the projects..."

"You mean Augustine's," said the cabbie, cranking up the radio to the blues station.

They were stomping their feet, shaking their heads, passing the joint – this time to the cabbie as well; it was just like every day all over again.

Augustine's was a large shed which looked like it could keel over at any time. It was already bursting with music and when they pushed the door open there was barely room to stand – all they could do was squeeze across to the bar, get some bourbon shots and dance.

The music was – again – the end of the world. There was this old black pig on the stage wearing a bright pink suit with a strange hat – looks like a Shriner, said Zack. He was calm as a cucumber but his blues licks were like flames driving everyone into a dancing frenzy. That's J.B. Hutto Pig from Chicago, someone said. And that's his wife, pointing at a woman pig who was spinning around in a trance.

Everybody was dancing with everybody, Pearlie got lost, Zack showed up with more bourbon shots and they all danced like the wild tchopitoulas pigs for what seemed like hours till, suddenly, the music stopped. The pig in the trance went up on the stage and tenderly wiped Hutto

Pig's face with her sweat-soaked chemise and helped him down.

Zack and Pearlie and Shri Vindaloo staggered out of the inferno and hung around for a bit, smoking a joint, till Zack said, "Let's take the streetcar home."

Arms linked they walked the couple of beautiful tree-lined blocks, Hutto Pig's madness replaced by the music of crickets and, wouldn't you know, just as they got to St. Charles, a streetcar creaked and clanged up.

"Best for last," said Pearlie as they clambered on and went to the seats at the back where they spread out across one another and let the sweat slowly evaporate as the streetcar squeakily wended its way uptown.

She was right. It was the best part of the day.

What Happened to the Pope?

The Pope was already in Bombay and was coming down to Goa the next day. The program for his two days in Goa was jam-packed – he would be arriving in the afternoon and immediately visiting the Church of St. Francis Xavier, and then an orphanage near Old Goa. The next day there was a small (ha ha) reception at the Cardinal's house and then a big public mass at the Parade Grounds in Panjim at which nearly 10 lakh people were expected, after which he was to fly out again.

Luiz and his mother and, joy of joys, Guadalupe had flown into Goa a few days earlier on their private plane. Shri Vindaloo and EunicePig had received them at the airport and immediately a plume of celebration filled the air.

Luiz was, of course, jumping out of his skin at seeing EunicePig. "Mama," he had EunicePig in a discreet side-embrace as he presented her to his mother, "this is my beautiful lovely wonderful EunicePig."

EunicePig was all smiles as she embraced Mama Lagarto, a strikingly elegant older pig with brilliant pink lipstick. Mama cheek-to-cheeked her and then held her at arm's length to look at her properly. "I see you are wearing our family earrings," she smiled approvingly. "And what a perfectly matched feather boa. Did you get it here in Goa?"

Shri Vindaloo, who had been shyly not-quite-nuzzling Guadalupe, took the cue and Mama Lagarto's paw, delivering his signature lighter-than-air kiss. "And, this is for you, Mama Lagarto," pulling out the lipstick pink boa from behind his back.

"Oh, that's lovely, thank you. How did you know I love pink?"

"I saw a picture of you at Luiz' home and knew that we were made for each other – pink is my favourite colour, too." He was dressed in almost all pink, with highlights of blue and green. "And for you, dear Guadalupe," draping her shoulders with the turquoise-midnight blue boa, noting her stunning pair of turquoise heels. There are no coincidences in life, he thought for the umpteenth time. "But none of these are from Goa," he said. "I got them in a dusty little boutique in the French Quarter in New Orleans."

Guadalupe pulled him back to her side and kissed his cheek rather close to his lips. "Thank you Shri Vindaloo. And how did you know I love New Orleans?"

"I didn't. In fact, I'd never even been there but I picked up the wrong boarding card when we bye-byed in Mexico City. And my friends, Zack and Pearlie Pig, showed me such a good time. What a great city – we should all go back there some day."

He returned her kiss and turned to his friend, "And for you Luiz, we have nothing …" pulling EunicePig and Luiz together, "…but a wonderful future."

They clambered into the waiting convertible carriage with Mama Lagarto sitting in the back with Shri Vindaloo, the two lovelies in the middle and Luiz in front with the driver.

"And how are Delicia and Paloma? It's a shame they couldn't come along."

"Oh, they were so disappointed," said Guadalupe. "They are falling out of their porkskins to meet you, Shri Vindaloo. But they have exams, and Miguel very kindly decided he would stay back and help them as they needed."

"A real gentleman," smiled Shri Vindaloo, turning to Mama Lagarto who had on an enigmatic look.

"And when do we meet the Holy Father?" she asked.

"He arrives in Goa tomorrow, I think." He looked at EunicePig, who nodded. "He is only here a couple of days, so has no time for any private audiences. Of course, we will all be seated in the front row at the Cardinal's reception. Maybe you could blow kisses at him, Mama Lagarto."

"Do you think that would be wise, Shri Vindaloo," she twinkled. "And please call me Juanita."

Luiz and Guadalupe looked at each other.

Shri Vindaloo half-bowed, smiling at her. He turned to Luiz. "Things have become a little more complicated since we last spoke, Luiz. Santan has returned to Goa…"

"Whaaaat? Oy!" from all the Mexicans, most loudly Luiz in the front seat.

EunicePig put one hand on his shoulder. "Santan and I have spoken, Luiz, and I've told him about our love, and he understands. In fact, he congratulated me. And so, while he is back in Goa, he will not be an obstacle to our marriage."

"He may even be able to help us," said Shri Vindaloo. "He has stopped drinking and is now working as the Cardinal's private chauffeur. His mother, Auntie Piedade, is very close to the Cardinal and she has already told him that Santan is happy with EunicePig marrying Luiz and she will be with us at the Cardinal's reception."

"But why didn't you tell us earlier, EunicePig." Mama Lagarto was frowning.

"I told her not to, Ma...Juanita," said Shri Vindaloo. "I knew that Luiz would have been very upset, and being so far away and not being able to do anything would have been horribly frustrating. When I got back to Goa and met with Auntie Piedade and Santan and EunicePig, I realized that Santan being here would be no problem at all for Luiz and EunicePig. However, the Cardinal said that, even for the Holy Father, things may be tricky. His hands are tied in so many ways since there are very strict rules for approving an annulment."

"The church really has no place for romance," said Mama Lagarto, shaking her head. "I sometimes feel it has no heart, which is why I have been exploring Buddhism recently."

Guadalupe and Luiz raised their eyebrows. "You never said anything about that, Mama."

"I have been thinking about this for a long time. We are Catholics and have been raised in the church for generations, and you two know how much we have done for the church in Mexico. But, as I look around and talk to people, I am beginning to feel that the church has no place for romance, no place for what people want. And I don't think the church is unique – all the religions I have read about are the same. They talk about the word of some God or another, but they don't think about people. What do you think Shri Vindaloo?"

"Juanita, you said it perfectly. I remember when I was recently in New York, I went into St. Patrick's Cathedral on Fifth Avenue, and there were all these people – dozens, maybe even a hundred – all of whom were walking around so down in the mouth. In such a glorious place. I couldn't understand it. It's a house of God – God never wants us to be down in the mouth – God is always tickling us so we can be happy!" He ended with a flourishing crescendo.

Guadalupe smiled but Luiz was unconvinced. "But what do we do if the Holy Father doesn't grant an annulment?"

"We'll find a solution, Luiz. Don't worry."

"And here we are at the Mandovi, the oldest hotel in Goa," said EunicePig. "My mother, Ermina, and Auntie Piedade, Santan's mother, will meet us here and we can all get to know each other properly."

"Look at that gorgeous river," Guadalupe whispered. "And what a romantic walkway."

"And tomorrow," EunicePig continued, "before the Holy Father arrives and Panjim gets completely crazy, we will move to the beach and stay at the mansion."

"Welcome to Goa," said Shri Vindaloo.

They entered the grand portal of the Mandovi and EunicePig went running ahead to her grey-haired, smiling mother and Aunty Piedade, also grey-haired and smiling. Both ladies were in saris. "Mummy, Aunty Piedade, this is Luiz' mother, Mama Lagarto, and his sister, Guadalupe and – best for last – my love, Luiz."

Ermina smiled and shook Mama Lagarto's hand a bit formally and then pulled Luiz into an oh-so-happy embrace. She was a large pig and Luiz found himself asmile in flesh. He came out of the embrace a little winded and happy as he could be. "Mama, it's so lovely to meet you and thank you so much for your incomprehensibly wonderful daughter. I will make her happy forever."

"It is already forever, Luiz," said EunicePig.

Aunty Piedade, equally Goan in her demeanour but a bit less shy, hugged EunicePig, "You are still my daughter, my darling. And Mama Lagarto..."

"Please call me Juanita, and may I call you Piedade?"

"Of course, as I was about to say, we now are a big international family."

Pulling Ermina in, the three older ladies performed a courtly embrace.

Shri Vindaloo and Guadalupe were watching this love-in, almost evaporating with joy.

"Ahhhh," breathed Shri Vindaloo quietly.

"Oh," was Guadalupe, slightly breathless.

The manager of the hotel came up to them, congratulated the happy couple and took charge of the check-in. Mama Lagarto had the Grand Suite with two bedrooms, one for her and Guadalupe, and one for Luiz; Shri Vindaloo and EunicePig had regular suites overlooking the river, all on the same floor. Auntie Piedade lived in Panjim and so would be going home that evening, and Ermina was staying with her for the night.

After the visitors washed up, they all met up at the first floor restaurant, where Shri Vindaloo had arranged a special dinner. The Mandovi did not, as a rule, serve feni, but had arranged some for Shri Vindaloo – caju feni for the pig men, and special kokum palm feni cocktails for the pig ladies.

There was a band playing a mix of old Konkani classics and, when it saw that Shri Vindaloo had some foreign guests, it shifted to some uptempo jazz ballads.

"Why don't you sing for us, EunicePig," said Mama Lagarto. "I understand you sing beautifully."

"Oh, do EunicePig," said Luiz very excited. "Mama, this is how I fell in love with her."

EunicePig looked around shyly at Shri Vindaloo who nodded barely perceptibly. She went up to the bandstand a little nervously, and, after a little back and forth with the band, took the mike. The violin took the lead and then the gentle rhythm section kicked in.

EunicePig looked straight at Luiz and sang:

At last...
my love has come along
my lonely days are over
and life is like a song...

Shri Vindaloo had to put his arm across Luiz' shoulder to keep him from falling off his chair. EunicePig was the best singer in Goa and she was in love.

Everyone in the restaurant stopped eating. Overwhelmed by the romance, many couples reached out to each other. When she finished, there was a stillness in the room, followed by whoops and cheers and joyous applause.

EunicePig was blushing, Luiz was blushing, Ermina and Aunty Piedade were beaming with pride, and Mama Lagarto had on the most beatific smile in the universe. Guadalupe, who sat on the other side of Shri Vindaloo, slid a bit closer in. Shri Vindaloo, took her paw, squeezing it gently.

By the time the food arrived, Shri Vindaloo had danced with Juanita, then Ermina, then Aunty Piedade and then, of course, with Guadalupe. Luiz and EunicePig danced like they were one.

The dinner was magnificent and afterwards, they took coffee on the verandah. Aunty Piedade and Ermina had to leave shortly after and Luiz and EunicePig took them down to the carriage that would ride them home. When they returned, Mama Lagarto said she was tired and they escorted her up to her suite. Guadalupe and Shri Vindaloo smiled at each other on the verandah.

"Can we take a walk by the river?" she asked softly.

"Welcome to Goa, Guadalupe," Shri Vindaloo said as they crossed the quiet street in front of the Mandovi and ambled slowly up the river walk.

"It's really special, Shri Vindaloo."

"You ain't seen nothing yet, my dear, as they say in America."

"You love America, don't you, Shri Vindaloo?"

"Oh, yes. I've only been there a few times, but it's just so much fun – there's always more going on and, in the words of the great American Saint, always more to come." He smiled at her. "But it's not Goa."

They were walking very close to each other and they could see the almost full moon shimmering on the river.

Conscious that she was married, Shri Vindaloo tried to blink away the cloud of romance that was starting to envelop them. "Your mother is such a star," he said. "She seems a lot like you."

"Well, I'd say I'm a lot like her."

"Except that she likes pink," he laughed. "And you love blue."

"Shri Vindaloo, you're so... so ..." Guadalupe was right up against him, her face lifted up to his.

It was impossible to resist. He kissed her, trying to think about Miguel and her kids, a losing proposition.

They sat down paw in paw on a nearby bench, her head on his shoulder. He tried again. "So, tell me the best thing about Delicia and Paloma."

"Oh, there's a thousand things, Shri Vindaloo. And one day – soon – you will meet them and see for yourself." And they kissed again. And again.

The moonlight on the river, the caju fenis, EunicePig's song and Guadalupe had Shri Vindaloo more than intoxicated. After a time, he stuttered out, "Your Mama must be tired."

Guadalupe looked at his heart, loving him even more. "You're right," she moved away slightly, "We should go back."

They walked back slowly, still enjoying the romantic perfume of the river. She leaned over and kissed him again as they reached the hotel.

In the lift they stood very close, touching each other. But no more.

By the time Shri Vindaloo got down for breakfast, the rest of the party was continuing the celebration on the verandah. He kissed the lady pigs and squeezed Luiz' shoulder. Juanita and Guadalupe were in earnest conversation with the hotel manager.

Juanita turned to him. "Shri Vindaloo, Custodio has been telling us that the Mandovi is up for sale."

"Yes, the owner passed away and his only son, Antonio, is a cabaret dancer in Paris and, much as he loves Goa, he feels he cannot return to live here. We have been keeping things afloat…"

"And you are doing an admirable job, Custodio."

"…looking for a buyer. You know the story, Shri Vindaloo."

"You know we have some hotels, Shri Vindaloo – you stayed in one in Mexico City where I took you when you arrived." Guadalupe was smiling at the memory. "We have nearly a dozen all across Mexico. And, we have just bought a hotel in Las Vegas, and I was telling Mama it would be great to buy the Mandovi as well."

"It certainly has excellent bones," said Juanita. "And with Guadalupe's special touch, we could bring her back to more than her original magic. My daughter, as you clearly already know, Shri Vindaloo, is quite a virtuoso pig."

"Ah, yes," Shri Vindaloo didn't have to be reminded – the river walk had played loud in his dreams.

"And, of course, Luiz would move here and manage it when he marries EunicePig."

"Praise the lord!" Shri Vindaloo smiled up at the heavens. "That would be such a splendid gift for me." He hadn't really thought about how he would have lived his life if EunicePig left Goa. And this also meant he'd be seeing a lot more of Guadalupe.

EunicePig was sitting very close to Luiz and smiling and smiling and smiling. "Mama Lagarto, what an amazing plan! And you will need to visit us often, and, of course, we will need to come to Mexico to see you and all the family."

"And I must see more of Ermina – she seems so lovely."

"Mummy *is* lovely," said EunicePig, "and you'll meet her again later today, and Aunty Piedade as well."

Luiz was leaning into EunicePig's hair and humming what sounded like a Konkani love song.

Juanita took Shri Vindaloo's paw and kissed it. "If I were twenty years younger…"

"You are," said Shri Vindaloo, as he tucked into his breakfast.

By the time they arrived at Shri Vindaloo's mansion by the beach it was nearly noon. Sarita greeted them, of course, with cooling towels and Shri Vindaloo introduced her but, of course, she mainly had eyes for Luiz and EunicePig for she had been, in a sense, the midwife of their love.

Ermina and Aunty Piedade were already there in the kitchen, putting the final touches on lunch. Sarita brought the drinks trolley out to the terrace, and Luiz, more at home in Goa by the minute, made some palm feni cocktails for his mother and Guadalupe – EunicePig was holding off for now – and, of course, two caju fenis for himself and Shri Vindaloo.

They all toasted what a glorious life it was and, of course, EunicePig and Luiz.

"What an elegant drink, Shri Vindaloo," said Mama Lagarto, smiling in her lounger under the palm trees. "It isn't like anything I've ever had before, although…"

"Juanita, palm feni is the smoothest drink you can get, particularly when it is mashed up into a cocktail by your son in love."

"It's different from caju feni, then?" said Guadalupe, a bit apprehensive since she remembered Shri Vindaloo telling her about how caju feni grows hair on your chest.

"Yes, dear Guadalupe. I'd say palm feni is like the best tequila and caju feni is like the roughest mescal. But both of them have magical qualities. Look at Luiz."

Luiz, who was already on his second drink, was glowing as if the sun was shining from behind his eyes. It was a beautiful day with a clear blue sky and the palm trees, of course, swaying in the breeze.

"These are my friends," said Shri Vindaloo, pointing to the trees. "I talk to them every day. Except I can't remember all of their names – that's Sylvester, I think, and there's Xavier." He waved at them. "They are all male, and If you listen closely, you can hear them sing."

"I can't hear anything," said Luiz.

"Listen closely, Luiz. Or ask EunicePig."

"I learned to sing listening to the palm trees, Luiz," she reached over and kissed him lightly on his cheek. "But, Shri Vindaloo, to me they sound female."

Juanita was smiling at the banter and the breeze. "Male, female, what does it matter – as long as they are happy. And," smiling at Shri Vindaloo, "they certainly look happy."

Ermina and Aunty Piedade came out to the terrace, announcing lunch. Ermina had changed into slacks and a top; Aunty Piedade, of course, wore a sari.

"I want to learn how to wear a sari," said Juanita, embracing the ladies in turn. "Where can I get one?"

"We can go to the market in the evening," said EunicePig, "but we'll also need to measure you up for a blouse. Mummy?"

"Of course," said Ermina. "I'll call the tailor to the house this evening."

"That would be wonderful, Ermina."

At lunch, the table was a celebration of what seemed like all of Goa – rava fried mussels, prawns recheado masala, oysters xacuti, chicken cafreal, and fish curry, rice, and pickles, and papad and poi and, of course, even more feni.

"What a grand feast," said Guadalupe, falling back in her chair. "Thank you."

"Goa is so much like Mexico, isn't it?" said Juanita.

"It is," said Shri Vindaloo. "I was right at home in Mexico."

"But you're right at home everywhere, Shri Vindaloo," said Luiz, helping his mother-in-law-to-be up from her chair.

Ermina took his arm and said gently, "Luiz, Aunty Piedade spoke to the Cardinal this morning..."

"And...?"

"Well, Luiz," said Aunty Piedade in a low voice, "I'm afraid he said it would be impossible to arrange the annulment."

"Oh no!" said Luiz. "But we were to see the Holy Father..."

"He said he didn't want to put the Holy Father in an embarrassing position. You see, not only are there no real grounds for an annulment, but since Santan works for the Cardinal, even if the Holy Father were to give an exemption, people would say..."

"Bah!" Juanita exploded. "Not just narrow-minded but driven by politics."

EunicePig had her arm around Luiz and Guadalupe walked over to her mother. Aunty Piedade and Ermina looked down at the floor.

Sarita came in. "Would anyone like some tea? Or coffee?"

"I'd love some tea, Sarita," said Juanita brightly.

Everyone looked at Shri Vindaloo, who was, of course, smiling.

"I can understand the Cardinal's dilemma," he said. "He's a truly good pig and close to us, but he is the face of the Church in Goa. But, no matter – we can fix this. My friend, Zack in New Orleans, is known as the Imperfect Master; we can ask him to create and conduct a special ceremony."

"The Imperfect Master? I've never heard of him, Shri Vindaloo, in all my studies." Juanita was leaning forward, very close to him.

"I, too, encountered him just recently, at the zydeco festival in Abbeville..."

"What's zydeco?" asked Luiz, confused between being upset and excited.

"Zydeco is the most amazing music – like mariachi, with the romance of Konkani songs multiplied by a rhythm that gets everyone, even people in wheelchairs, dancing. It was amazing…but, more than the music and the dancing and…oh all kinds of other things, I met this long-haired pig who had travelled around India. He told me about the Imperfect Master who is a special human incarnation of the Buddha"

Juanita was nodding. "The Perfect Master."

"Yes, Juanita, but this is the Imperfect Master – Buddha without a brain. The strange pig pointed out that the brain, as we all know, is a useful tool – 7 + 7 = 14 or 15 or whatever – but it can't help you find joy. The Imperfect Master has all the wonderful attributes of the Buddha and also recognizes that none of us is perfect. We all make mistakes, which means that we, like everyone else, truly belong in the kingdom of God – there is no narrow-mindedness in the Imperfect Master, no politics, only a smiling focus on what we need and want. Just like you said, Juanita."

Juanita almost kissed him. "This is so fantastic, Shri Vindaloo."

Shri Vindaloo nodded, EunicePig and Guadalupe smiled in delight, and even Luiz, who still looked confused, was beginning to cheer up.

"Does the Imperfect Master have a church? Or a temple?" Aunty Piedade was stretching her belief to imbibe this new happiness.

"No, No, Aunty Piedade. There's no church, no temple, no rent to pay, no rules to follow. Zack, the Imperfect

Master, is like any of us – he lives his life, he does business, he dances to zydeco and he makes mistakes, of course, which God forgives – it's just life, which is only about love."

"And joy," said EunicePig. Shri Vindaloo had already spoken to her about Zack and Pearlie, but not from this ecclesiastic angle. She trusted Shri Vindaloo completely and her mother, of course, loved her daughter. Aunty Piedade would come around.

Juanita kissed her son, who was slowly beginning to believe.

"The only thing," continued Shri Vindaloo, "is that the wedding will have to be somewhere other than Goa."

"Didn't you say your friend, Zack, is in New Orleans," Guadalupe was smiling. "I love New Orleans."

"Darling, why don't we do the wedding at our new hotel in Las Vegas?"

"Juanita, that would be fantastic," said Shri Vindaloo. "I was to go to Vegas on my last trip to America but it got turned upside down. That would be perfect. No, I should say, perfectly imperfect."

They all laughed, including Aunty Piedade and Luiz.

"Let me call Zack right now."

"And I will call the tailor," said Ermina.

Ermina, Aunty Piedade and EunicePig took Juanita to the village market, and Shri Vindaloo took Luis and Guadalupe to the beach.

He had never seen Guadalupe in a swimsuit before. It made him a bit dizzy; swaying in the breeze like one of his palm tree friends; he started singing a squawky abstract love song and plunged into the waves. He came up sputtering and Guadalupe and Luiz were laughing all around him – Mexico and Goa were one.

They had a wonderful afternoon and by the time they returned to the mansion, the ladies were back, proudly displaying their shopping. Aunty Piedade had bought Juanita a lovely pink (of course) chiffon sari, and three contrasting blouse pieces, and Juanita had picked up some typical Goan embroidered cushion covers. The tailor was on his way to measure her up for the blouses.

Aunty Piedade had to get back to Panjim to be ready for the madness of the Pope's visit and EunicePig took Luiz and his mother to her mother's house for tea. Shri Vindaloo and Guadalupe were left alone on the verandah, still in their swimsuits. Sarita had brought them tea and gone back downstairs.

The sun was setting as Guadalupe reached over for Shri Vindaloo's paw. He shifted his lounger closer to hers and they lay silently side by side watching the sun slip slowly down towards the horizon.

"Shri Vindaloo," she began. He kissed her paw.

She lifted her sunglasses and he could see her extraordinarily beautiful eyes were smiling but with a vulnerability he had never seen before. "I have to tell you something about Miguel."

"Guadalupe," Shri Vindaloo took both her paws in his and kissed each in turn. "What is it? Is everything alright with your family?"

She suddenly laughed. "Oh, my family – our family – is fine. It's just that over the past few years, Miguel has changed ..."

"How do you mean? He still loves you, I assume."

"Oh, yes, he does. But he's been...how do I say it ... exploring an alternative sexuality. And, now he has decided to go through gender reassignment surgery."

Shri Vindaloo's eyes widened. With a start, he dropped Guadalupe's paws, but quickly took them up again.

"But, what about you? What about Delicia and Paloma?"

"Oh, the kids love Miguel. And he loves them, of course. And me. But...he has to follow his dreams. And I,...I feel so lucky to have met you, Shri Vindaloo."

He pulled her closer to him, embracing her tenderly.

"And I you, Guadalupe." They kissed like first-time lovers, eagerly and with increasing passion till they almost tumbled off the loungers. "We are just so blessed."

"We *are*, Shri Vindaloo, and now that Luiz will be living in Goa with EunicePig..."

"And the Mandovi will bring you back to us more and more. But I must meet the little piggies. And Miguel. Maybe I should come back to Mexico City with you."

"I think not now," Guadalupe pulled back to talk to him more seriously. "Miguel's treatment is in its last rounds. And the kids have to settle into it too. So, I don't want to confuse them, bringing you into the picture right now. Although they are desperately keen to meet you."

"Never a dull moment with you, my darling," said Shri Vindaloo.

"That's certainly the truth. And you still don't know all of it. We bought the hotel in Las Vegas so that Miguel – he goes by Micaela now – could host a show there. He is a tall, good looking pig and we had a great relationship, or so I thought. One day, a little over a year ago, I came home late from work and he greeted me dressed in a glittering long black gown. I was shocked, although I must say he made a super-hot lady pig."

"Where were Delicia and Paloma?"

"They were asleep. He told me that he had been to a couple of drag shows recently and found that he really loved them and then started experimenting with dressing up."

They were sitting knee-to-knee on the loungers facing each other. Shri Vindaloo kissed her eyelids.

"I was so confused...terrified in a sense. I didn't know what to say. I suddenly realized that our physical intimacy had been drifting away slowly over the previous few months. I hadn't thought anything of it – I had been very busy at work and he with taking care of the kids. But I must say, he looked beautiful – he had glitter on his eyelids and bright crimson lipstick – you'd have loved it, Shri Vindaloo."

He smiled, kissing her again.

"He was a great husband – he still is, really. We were quite a star couple in Mexico City. He danced like a dream – rather like you do. And he was always so thoughtful.

And sexy – again, like you are. And with the babies he was always beyond wonderful. And it kept getting better as they grew up."

"How are you explaining this new papa to them?"

"Nothing's really different as yet. They call him Papa, and when he dresses up, they call him Papi – it's a game to them…"

"It *is* a game, though," said Shri Vindaloo, caressing her under her chin. "Everything in life is."

"I worry, though, that once the surgery kicks in, things may change. And as word gets out…"

"Well, you all still love each other, right?"

"Absolutely," said Guadalupe definitively. "Except, now I also have you." This time she kissed him and pulled him to her as she lay back on the lounger.

Sarita came running onto the terrace, "Uh…uh…Shri Vindaloo, madam is back."

They jumped up, Guadalupe straightening her swimsuit.

"But what about Juanita?" he asked her.

"As you saw, she's even more modern that I am."

Juanita and Luiz came smiling out onto the terrace.

"We had such a great time – Ermina and EunicePig are just as sweet as they could be. Shri Vindaloo, thank you again for bringing such joy to our family."

"Where is EunicePig?"

"She's decided to stay with her mother tonight – once more an almost-married pig," said Luiz, smiling. "She said we have an early start tomorrow."

"So we do," said Shri Vindaloo. "But I think a caju feni or two may be a necessary ticket right now, if only to salute the magical sunset we just saw."

"Oh, of course," said Luiz and signalled Sarita with a flying kiss.

It turned into a lovely, quiet at-home evening, with Juanita regaling Shri Vindaloo with some not-quite-modest tales of her youth, some of which were new even to her children.

"If I were just twenty years older..." said Shri Vindaloo. He kissed her paw, hugged Luiz, and kissed Guadalupe's cheek a little less discreetly, as they finally went to bed.

Shri Vindaloo was dreaming that Guadalupe was in his bed as a New Orleans Swing Jazz band played on the terrace. His paws rose and fell as he mock played the trombone, and, to his amazement he woke to find that Guadalupe *was* in his bed, and naked at that.

His outstretched paws enveloped her as the number came to an end and they kissed.

"Guadalupe," he breathed.

"Shhhh," she smiled at him.

A different music rose gently, sweetly persistently. They were like long-time lovers – they *were* long-time lovers, feeling, tasting, kissing each other till a passion from their history took over.

After what seemed like hours, they subsided into each other's arms, grunting quietly. They lay in bed and looked up at the moon. Shri Vindaloo had become a joyous smile.

Guadalupe kissed him, rising up on her elbow. "I must go back to my room, my darling. I love you."

"Not yet, my love."

More music – it sounded like zydeco – began to play, and Guadalupe turned more tempestuous than ever. They made love again for what seemed like forever, the bedclothes flew across the room, and they ended up naked on the terrace, holding each other as dawn was breaking.

"Shri Vindaloo, I really must go now – someone may see me coming out of your bedchamber."

"This is where you belong, my love."

She collected her robe from the pile-up on the floor and they kissed more tenderly than ever at the door.

"Good night, darling."

His smile followed her down the corridor to her room.

It seemed like just a few minutes later that Sarita was knocking on his door.

"Shri Vindaloo, our guests are already at breakfast. Are you ready? You have to leave for the Pope's reception soon."

"Oh, Sarita, thank you, my dear." He rubbed his eyes, trying to think quickly. "Can you get the pink and blue toga – the one I wore during Carnival last year – ironed and bring it to me, please. And, of course, some of your special magic coconut coffee."

He made it to the verandah just in time – late, of course, but just in time.

"My God, Shri Vindaloo," said Juanita, "you look like you'll upstage the Pope."

"Just doing my job, Juanita. But you all look mighty festive and tasty yourselves." Juanita was in a pink shift with an orange throw shawl, and Guadalupe wore a fitted navy and turquoise dress that reminded him of the previous night. Luiz was in a fine linen suit with, of course, a slightly sombrero-ey straw hat – truly Senor Lagarto.

Shri Vindaloo sat down next to Guadalupe, who still had stars in her eyes. He began to sing – *la deee de da dee deeeeee*. She smiled, looking lovelier than he had ever seen her – indeed, lovelier than he had ever seen anyone before.

Juanita could tell that something was up but she discreetly looked away and said, "Luiz, the pilot called and said that the airport closes at 6:30 pm since it has to be cleared for the Pope's flight."

Guadalupe shook her head, pulling away from Shri Vindaloo. "That means we'll have to leave by around 3 or 4 in the afternoon."

Luiz looked downcast. "I can't believe we have to leave today."

Guadalupe reached out to cheer him up. "But it won't be long now, Luiz. Soon, you and EunicePig will be..."

"But when, Guadalupe, when?" plaintively.

"You know we have to see how Miguel's program is working – I'm pretty sure it won't be more than a couple of months."

"Luiz," said Shri Vindaloo, "I spoke to Zack yesterday, and he will, of course, be delighted to conduct the wedding. I told him it would probably be in Las Vegas, which delighted him even more. He's sniffing around to find a perfectly imperfect wedding chapel."

Ermina and EunicePig arrived in a rush. "We're late, we must leave now."

Luiz smiled at his mother-in-law-to-be and embraced EunicePig. "Darling, we have to leave this afternoon, but…"

"This afternoon?" EunicePig held on to him like she couldn't let him go.

Juanita came up and put her arms around both of them. "Darlings, we have to go back to take care of a few things as quickly as we can so we can fix the wedding as soon as possible."

Shri Vindaloo joined the huddle. "It will be in Las Vegas. And it will be amay-zing."

They had to scurry out as it was now getting really late for the Pope's reception.

The traffic was horrendous and by the time they got to the Cardinal's house it was a good thing that Aunty Piedade and Santan were at the gate to escort/hurry them through.

EunicePig introduced Santan, who was in the Cardinal's chauffeur's regalia, to Luiz first, and then to his mother and sister.

There was no hiding from the fact that he was a good-looking Goan pig. Shri Vindaloo remembered him well, but his usually dark, flashing eyes, which had obviously caught EunicePig's attention when they were all younger, appeared to have flattened out.

He smiled politely at the company and told Luiz, "Congratulations Luiz, I know you will be very happy with EunicePig."

Aunty Piedade hurried them in the side door to their seats in the front row of the reception hall just as the Cardinal made his entrance.

Shri Vindaloo sat with Juanita on one side and EunicePig on the other; Luiz was next to his betrothed with Ermina and Aunty Piedade alongside. Guadalupe was next to her mother, which was perhaps best, given the electric attraction between her and Shri Vindaloo.

The Cardinal smiled at their party and Aunty Piedade nodded signalling to him that she had communicated the situation to all of them.

"A blessed morning to you all," the Cardinal began his address, "but I'm sorry to inform you that His Holiness is a little under the weather this morning, and, given the huge crowds that are already lining up for the Mass at the Parade Grounds, he decided that he would need to give this morning's reception a miss. He apologizes to you all profusely and, of course, offers his blessings."

There was disappointed murmuring around the room.

Juanita was more than a little miffed, "We came all the way from Mexico to see the Pope..."

"But look what you got instead," said Shri Vindaloo, pointing to the lovebirds sitting by her.

"That's true," she said, smiling happily. "But still…"

The Cardinal came over to them. "Good morning, Shri Vindaloo, I'm sorry for this disappointment."

"I hope the Holy Father feels better; maybe he needs some caju feni," Shri Vindaloo smiled at him. The Cardinal shook his head indulgently. "And this is Madame Juanita Lagarto from Mexico; Juanita, this is Cardinal Gomes, a kind and, I would say, very modern figure in the Goan church."

Juanita kissed his ring. "It is a disappointment, Cardinal Gomes, but I suppose it can't be helped."

He nodded, smiling and stepped over to EunicePig. "Ah, EunicePig, my favourite songbird, and this must be Luiz – I understand some sort of congratulations are in order, even though…"

"I have explained it all to them," interjected Aunty Piedade quickly.

"But I can certainly extend my personal blessings," said the gracious Cardinal, "and I can hope that one day I will hear EunicePig's *Ave Maria* again."

They kissed his ring in turn and he moved on to the next family in the front row.

Mother-henning them, Aunty Piedade said, "The Cardinal has told Santan to provide us an escort in his car to enable us to get through the throngs. Do we need to go back to Shri Vindaloo's place?"

"That's very thoughtful of him," said Shri Vindaloo. "But why don't we go to the Mandovi, since, in any case, we will have to leave for the airport in a couple of hours."

Shri Vindaloo and Juanita joined Aunty Piedade in the Cardinal's car which led the way through the screaming traffic so they got to the Mandovi – normally a ten-minute ride – in just under a half hour.

Shri Vindaloo congratulated Santan on how he had turned his life around. "And you're happy now?" he asked.

Santan smiled across at him beatifically. "My mother and the Lord Jesus Christ saved me, Shri Vindaloo. And I have to thank you for taking care of EunicePig, who I treated so badly."

"She's very happy, Santan, so all's well."

"But, do you know what happened to His Holiness?" asked Juanita. "Will he be well enough for the Mass?"

"Well," he began "..."

"Santan!" Aunty Piedade said sharply.

"No, no, tell us. Please."

"He was quite well yesterday," said Santan, "but for dinner, they had some fish recheado masala and prawn balchow that I think didn't go down very well with the Holy Father, and the Cardinal said he was a bit uncomfortable this morning."

"Oh...oh dear," said Juanita, smiling to herself.

"I'm sure he'll be well by the afternoon," said Shri Vindaloo suppressing his own smile, as they pulled into the Mandovi.

He escorted the ladies in and found Luiz and EunicePig in discussion with Custodio. Juanita joined them and Shri Vindaloo and Guadalupe took another stroll by the river.

Viva Las Vegas

Shri Vindaloo, EunicePig and Ermina arrived in Las Vegas a few days before the rest of the party. They were received with great fanfare at the Hotel Malaguena, as they were guests of the Lagarto family who owned the hotel.

Shri Vindaloo was shown into a grand suite, larger than any he had stayed in before, and, in addition to a gorgeous arrangement of flowers, there was a bottle of tequila and one of mescal on the table AND a welcome note signed with lipstick marks. The hotel was at the bottom edge of the Strip and out his window he could see miles and miles and miles of neon and then sky. EunicePig and Ermina came in raving about their room as well.

They had a champagne toast with Jimmy the Pig, the manager of the hotel, and then rushed downstairs. Shri Vindaloo wanted to see, smell, feel the casino, and smile wide-eyed at the scantily-dressed lady pigs, many of whom had feathers out of the rear side of their garments. It was a strange American paradise.

He also wanted to play poker and the manager escorted them to the Lagarto Poker Playa, which was a well-appointed smoke-filled room with a bar running along one side and six tables in pairs, crowded with poker players and their "lucks"; several sexy young pigs with feathered butts wandered around the room with cocktail trays. Shri Vindaloo whooped with delight and sidled up to a table to figure out what was going on – they were playing Texas Hold'em, which was new to him. He was used to playing five card stud, so he couldn't quite follow why there were all these cards open on the table, when he suddenly heard a loud, familiar voice.

"Shri Vindaloo, welcome to Las Vegas!"

He looked around and, wouldn't you know, it was Patty Pig who took such good care of him in the desert, and with her was Pig Dog, his friend from Garcia's.

"Patty! Pig Dog! How great to see you." But then, suddenly nervous, he looked around furtively.

Patty burst out laughing. "You don't need to worry, Shri Vindaloo, Duane ain't here." She peeled herself away from the table where she was Pig Dog's good luck charm, and threw herself on him, hugging and kissing him with delight.

Pig Dog got up from the table nodding to the dealer to hold his chips. He embraced Shri Vindaloo, "Great to see you, pardner. Let's go get cocktails."

They went to the bar at the side of the room. "Tequila sunrises all around," said Shri Vindaloo.

"With shots on the side," added Pig Dog.

"Patty, Pig Dog, this is EunicePig, and we're here in Las Vegas for her wedding, and this is her mother, Ermina."

"Congratulations EunicePig!" said Patty.

Pig Dog touched his cowboy hat. "Congratulations ma'am."

"Thank you," smiled EunicePig at both of them.

"And are you the lucky pig, Shri Vindaloo?"

"No," EunicePig smiled even more sweetly at him. "Shri Vindaloo is not my love. Although I do love him. Of course."

"Who doesn't?" said Patty, who was sitting right by him, very close. She patted his paw. "Well, I take that back – Duane didn't, for damn sure. But I think he'd be quite happy to see him right now, whadd'ya think, Pig Dog?"

EunicePig, of course, knew the story, but Ermina was looking lost. So Patty told her how she met Shri Vindaloo in New York and how he came out to the desert to visit her and how, Duane, her main – and only – pig at the time, got really upset.

"What do you mean, Patty – at the time? Have thing's changed?"

"Well, darling," she reached out her other paw to Pig Dog. "I got me a new pig dog – a real, swell one." She leaned over and kissed Pig Dog, who blushed prettily, particularly for such a big man.

"That's wonderful! But, what happened with Duane? He couldn't be too pleased with this."

"It's a real funny story..."

"But first," Pig Dog smiled, picking up his shot glass. "Welcome to America, ya'll."

They drained their shots, Ermina coughing gamely. Pig Dog signaled the waiter who brought the bottle and refilled their shot glasses.

"I don't think Mama and I will have shots," said EunicePig, "but the tequila sunrises are quite lovely."

"So, what happened with Duane?"

Patty was already laughing. "Well, it must have been six..." looking at Pig Dog, "no eight months ago, that Duane and I went to LA – believe it or not, my publisher in New York sent my manuscript to an agent friend of his in LA, who is pushing to make a movie of it..."

"Wow! Can I get a role?"

"Shri Vindaloo, you don't need a role in any movie – you are a movie. But, hey, like I told you, the book is about two pigs who meet in a bar, just like we did at Grand Central, so.... but, anyhoo, Duane came along with me since he had a day off from the ranch and, after our adventure – or, should I say, misadventure," pointing to Shri Vindaloo and herself, "he wouldn't let me go off anywhere by myself."

Pig Dog poured another round of shots.

"So, we get to LA and were a little early for the meeting, so we park the truck and wander out onto Rodeo Drive, and there, as if waiting for us, was a pack of Hare Krishna's..."

"Hare Krishna's? Indians? In LA?"

"Nah, they weren't Indians," looking at EunicePig and Ermina, "not at all like you guys – the Hare Krishnas were

Americans in these orange robes and had bells and whatnot and were singing and chanting…"

"Hare Krishna," sang Shri Vindaloo, "Hare Rama."

"You got it. I'd met some before in New York, so I tried to get away from them, but Duane was, surprisingly, quite taken with them…"

"Must have been that Ma Rainey, or whatever," piped in Pig Dog.

"Well, there was a very pretty young Hare Krishna thing, who was singing to Duane, and before I knew it, he was skipping and dancing like a fool in a cowboy hat."

"Must have looked hilarious," said Shri Vindaloo.

Patty and Pig Dog were laughing.

"I was amused but getting impatient, so I told him to c'mon so we could go look in the shop windows. But he was really getting into it and after maybe fifteen minutes, he came up to me and said, 'Patty, darlin' I'm sorry, but I've gotta go with them.' I was shocked. I didn't know what to say, but he just touched his paw to his lips and then mine – I'd never EVER seen him do anything so delicate – and then waltzed off, and that's the last I've seen of him."

Pig Dog said, "He called me after a week and told me he was happier than he's ever been, and he asked me to apologize to Patty and to get his things from the ranch and send them to the aash-ram. So I did," smiling, "and in ten minutes, Patty was in my life," and pulling her to him again.

Shri Vindaloo smiled knowingly at him. "I could tell you had a thing for her even back then."

"Of course, who didn't? You did, too, Shri Vindaloo."

"Of course, and I always will. But hey, you two look made for each other, don't they, EunicePig?"

"Well, now that I know what love is," said EunicePig, "I'd say that looks pretty close."

"And where is your lucky pig, EunicePig?" asked Patty.

"Ah, Luiz... I met him in Goa, through Shri Vindaloo, of course... he's on his way here from Mexico – and," clearly very excited, "he'll be here tomorrow."

Ermina smiled at them. "You must both must stay for the wedding, which is the day after tomorrow."

"Of course," said Patty, "we wouldn't miss if for the world."

"Fantastic!" said Shri Vindaloo, "But now I need to play some poker."

"Whyn't you take my seat and my chips," said Pig Dog, "and Patty darling you can sit by him and bring him luck – but..." wagging his finger with a smile, "nothing more – I know how smooth this fella is. Meanwhile, I'll take the ladies into the main casino and show them around."

He tipped his cowboy hat back on his head, and with the two beauties, one on each side, he strutted into the main hall.

Shri Vindaloo took his seat and saw that Pig Dog had built quite a pile of chips. Patty held his paw and tried to explain the details of the game to him. He nodded sagely and, slowly peeking at the two cards he was dealt, gave a sudden whoop. Everybody at the table looked at him – in fact, people from the next table looked over.

The first player on the dealers left checked, the second one bet some chips (twenty dollars, Patty whispered), the next two folded, the next one (on Shri Vindaloo's right) called, Shri Vindaloo called as did the last player (on the dealer's right); the first player folded, leaving four of them in the pot.

Shri Vindaloo smiled sillily and waited for the flop; when it came down, he whooped again, albeit a bit less loudly, and pushed about half of the chips in front of him into the pot. The dealer told him it wasn't his turn yet, but, by then, the other players, confounded by this strange beast, all folded their cards. Shri Vindaloo burst into a delighted laugh and, contrary to most practice, showed his hole cards – the two of diamonds and the six of spades, which with the open Jack of hearts, three of spades and the ten of clubs, added up to a big nothing.

Shri Vindaloo reached across and kissed Patty, delighted although he had won all of sixty dollars.

The next hand ran almost the same way – Shri Vindaloo whooping when he saw his hole cards, calling every bet, whooping again when the flop came down – the ten of diamonds, seven of spades and Jack of diamonds – and betting half his chips (this time when it was his turn). There were two players bold enough to call him. When the turn came – the three of clubs – Shri Vindaloo was uncharacteristically modest; it was his turn and he checked, as did all the others. At the fifth card – the Ace of diamonds – he whooped wildly; the player on his left looked at him as if he were insane and bet a stack of chips (two hundred and fifty dollars, whispered Patty). The other player folded and Shri Vindaloo, almost jumping out of his seat, pushed all his chips into the pot; the dealer counted out to total. His neighbor said he couldn't match the bet, but since it was table stakes, he called putting in all the chips he had.

Shri Vindaloo proudly turned over two black Aces and reached for the pot, but his neighbor tapped his paw, "Not so fast, my friend" and, smiling, tabled the King and three of diamonds, filling an Ace King Jack flush.

"Wow!" said Shri Vindaloo, "Look at that. Well done, my friend."

"Sorry 'bout that, pardner," said the winning pig.

"Oh, it was great," said Shri Vindaloo.

"But you lost," said Patty.

"Oh, but I won the first hand. I told you I always win – it's my poker face."

She laughed out loud. "But you lost far more than you won."

"Ah, but I don't play poker to make money – I play poker to have fun. Except that I've already lost some of Pig Dog's winnings – maybe we should go over and find them. Hasta la vista, guys."

He got up, giving Patty a squeeze and a kiss and they wandered paw-in-paw towards the main casino.

They found EunicePig telling Pig Dog some Goa tales while Ermina was deeply engrossed in a slot machine. As they came up to them, the slot maching hit a jackpot and coins poured out onto Ermina's lap and the floor.

"Welcome to Las Vegas, Ermina," said Pig Dog as he helped her pick up her coins. "I think this calls for champagne," looking around. A sexy feathered pig was there almost instantly with a tray of champagne coupes.

They toasted each other and life, and Ermina got back to the slot machine.

"Zack and Pearlie should be coming in about now," said EunicePig, as they heard a delighted, delicious screech and Pearlie came flying through the crowd and threw herself on Shri Vindaloo, kissing him like she was Zack's girlfriend but wasn't.

The drama even got Ermina off the slot machine. Shri Vindaloo introduced everyone around.

Zack, who had the imperfect master talisman on a chain around his neck and had grown a moustache, sang out, "Viva Las Vegas!"

"I see the imperfect master's still with you, Zack," said Shri Vindaloo, fondling the little Buddha.

"Haven't taken him off since you put it there, my friend. The imperfect master is always with me – when I sleep, when I shower, even when I make love."

"And he makes the most perfectly imperfect love you could imagine, Shri Vindaloo." Pearlie giggled, "Maybe you could join us some time – it is Vegas, after all."

"Thanks for the thought, Pearlie, but ..."

"You gettin' shy, Shri Vindaloo?" said Pearlie. "Remember the greatest Margarita in the world? And the Cajun girl in Abbeville?"

"And what 'bout me?" said Patty.

"Well," Shri Vindaloo smiled, "I still love all of you. But it's EunicePig's wedding and there's a lot to do."

Ermina had turned back to the slot machines and, delight of delights, hit another jackpot, albeit somewhat smaller. Pig Dog helped her pick up her chips, and convinced her to join them as they all moved towards the main bar, where the manager of the hotel welcomed them.

Shri Vindaloo greeted him. "Jimmy the Pig, this is some more of our wedding party."

"I know, I already met them, except for…"

"This is Patty and Pig Dog, old friends of mine from California – we met in the Lagarto Poker Playa."

"We weren't planning on staying," said Pig Dog. "We were going to drive back home tonight and come back for the wedding."

"No, no, you have to be here" said Shri Vindaloo, and Jimmy the Pig signaled to an assistant standing by.

"It's all arranged," he said.

Ermina, who was coming into flower, said, "It's time for another toast – perhaps champagne this time."

Zack took Ermina by the paw, "Congratulations to the lovely – and lucky, I see – mother of the bride." With his other paw, he reached out to EunicePig. "And what a bride?" He kissed her cheek, tickling her lips with his moustache.

Pearlie pulled all three of them into an embrace. "Ermina, congratulations. And EunicePig, I feel like I know you already. Shri Vindaloo told us about how you and Luiz met, how you and Luiz fell in love – and now, you and Luiz are getting married – it's perfect. Congratulations!"

They all cocktail-partied for a while, swishing this way and that.

Patty said, "We need to go shopping – we ain't dressed for a wedding. And we need to check into our suite."

"OK," said Shri Vindaloo, "and why don't we all reconnect in a couple of hours – I've got tickets for this amazing circus act at five in the hotel next door."

"A circus? In a hotel?" Even Zack, cooler than ever with his moustache, was amazed.

"It's called the Cirque de Soleil, or something, and Jimmy the Pig told me it's magical – to be seen to be believed."

"That sound's great," said Pearlie, "I love circuses."

"I think we'll pass," said Patty. "We'll stay in and enjoy the jacuzzi in our suite – after all, we're like newlyweds ourselves."

Shri Vindaloo air-kissed them both as they slipped off.

The circus was, indeed, amazing, magical, incomprehensibly more than any circus any of them had ever seen. First off, it was indoors in this amazing hotel; it was a modern circus and had no animals, but it had extraordinarily beautiful trapeze artists, strong pigs, midgets, giants, jugglers, clowns, balloons, and the wildest music and lights any of them had ever seen.

And then, for the *piece de resistance*, the ringmaster looked around the audience for volunteers and, of course, landed on Shri Vindaloo and Pearlie who were laughing and giggling and jumping up and down.

They went into the center of the ring, bowing like the stars they were, but then they froze up – slightly. Pearlie was delivered into the strong embrace of a French muscleman – she giggled at him and he rolled his lips in a very French manner.

Shri Vindaloo was escorted up a very, very, very tall ladder by a very, very, very sexy trapeze pig. The trapeze pig, who did speak a little English, kissed Shri Vindaloo on his snout and told him not to worry. She locked him into a harness and told him she would make sure he would be able to deliver hot, passionate kisses to his darling waiting on the ground.

The stage was set and the audience was stilled to silence. The band started with a drum roll and at the crash of the cymbal, the trapeze pig, much stronger than her slim frame looked, grasped Shri Vindaloo firmly by his buttocks as they whooshed through the air.

One, and back.

Two, and back.

Three, and whee! She spun head over heels in the air, keeping Shri Vindaloo in her deliciously tight embrace and, wonder of wonders, landed him with a not-too-gentle thrust onto Pearlie, who was leaning back in the embrace of the muscleman and screaming and shrieking in delight.

Shri Vindaloo was giddy and tottering. All he could say was, "Bhh..bhh..bh..th..thank you darling – I love your long fingernails."

The entire audience was on their feet in applause as Shri Vindaloo and Pearlie, breathing heavily staggered out of the arena. Zack, Ermina and EunicePig were wowed.

"We need drinks," said Zack.

They had a few rounds of Old Fashioneds while Shri Vindaloo caught his breath. Pearlie was still jumping around, but they decided to call it a day and return to the hotel. The Lagarto familia were coming in early the next day, and Shri Vindaloo was going to the airport to collect them with Jimmy the Pig; EunicePig and her Mama needed to rest before the big day; and Pearlie needed to take Zack to bed.

The next morning Shri Vindaloo took a stretch limousine from to the airport with Jimmy the Pig, who had arranged for the car to drive directly onto the tarmac. The plane landed just as they pulled up and Shri Vindaloo turned into a delighted smile as the familia Lagarto came down the airstairs.

In tune with his delight, Guadalupe was first off the plane, holding the two little piggies by their paws; both of them were wearing matching printed dresses. And wonder of wonders, their dresses had the same print as his shirt. Shri Vindaloo shouted out, "Ay caramba!"

EunicePig, he thought, smiling. She had, as she often did, bought him the hathi-ghoda-palkhi print fabric and had a shirt made by Fader, his tailor in Goa. How perfect –

she sent the same fabric to Guadalupe, who – even lovelier
– made it into the best possible surprise for everyone.

Guadalupe blew him a kiss as all three scampered down
the stairs and ran upto him. He embraced Guadalupe with
a half-passionate half-clumsy kiss, as he also grabbed the
piglets one in each arm and whirled them around. Delicia
and Paloma squealed in delight.

"And you are…" said Shri Vindaloo looking from one to
the other.

"I am Delicia," said the littler one, "and this is Paloma."

"Ooooh! you are both so lovely. And look, we have the
same shirts. It's magic!"

"It is, it is…" said Delicia; Paloma nodded up and down
enthusiastically.

He set them down and saw – my God, what a beautiful
family – Juanita, looking even sexier than she did in Goa;
Luiz, even more the old school Mexican gentleman pig,
complete with linen suit and cravat; and, as if that weren't
enough, this extraordinary, tall, voluptuous, more-than-
lady pig in a red satin sheath dress, displaying charms that
he could hardly believe.

"Papi, Papi," Delicia and Paloma ran upto her, crying
out almost in unison, "this is Shri Vindaloo – we have the
same shirts. It's magic!"

Guadalupe still had Shri Vindaloo in a half-embrace.
"Shri Vindaloo, this is Micaela, my – uh – husband."

Micaela reached down and kissed Shri Vindaloo on the
cheek, whispering, "Thank you, Shri Vindaloo, for loving
Guadalupe." They smiled at each other.

"Welcome to Las Vegas, Micaela, all of you."

"We should be welcoming you to Vegas, Shri Vindaloo," smiled Juanita, as she took his arm.

"Juanita, you look lovelier and – dare I say it – sexier than you did in Goa."

"Shri Vindaloo, you're too young for me."

"But I love older women," turning to smile at Guadalupe. "Actually I love all women."

"We know that, Shri Vindaloo," said Guadalupe. "And Mama certainly is a beauty."

Luiz suddenly piped up, "But where is EunicePig?"

"You can't see the bride the day before the wedding, Luiz – its bad luck," Guadalupe teased.

"But..but..."

"Don't worry, sir, she is waiting for you at the hotel with her mother," said Jimmy the Pig. "Let's get in the car."

It was a grand limousine with (almost) enough room for Delicia and Paloma to run around. They took turns jumping onto Shri Vindaloo's lap to match their dress with his shirt. Micaela reached out to them and Paloma jumped over to his lap, then Delicia and Paloma traded laps, and then again, and then again. Guadalupe, Juanita and Luiz laughed enjoying the show.

And then, Micaela started to sing.

La Cucaracha, la cucaracha
Ya no puede carminar...

Delicia and Paloma joined in the chorus, and then all the others, including Shri Vindaloo, who sang 'la cucaracha, la cucaracha, la dee la dee la dee dah' over and over again.

After a bit, Delicia and Paloma had calmed down a bit and squeezed themselves between their mother and their grandmother.

The limousine was approaching the hotel and Luiz started clapping his hands excitedly.

EunicePig and Ermina were waiting on the porch – Luiz jumped out even before the limousine stopped and raced to her. "My love," his eyes were closed and his head was moving from side to side kissing one cheek and then the other.

Delicia and Paloma were running forward in a line with Shri Vindaloo at one end and Micaela at the other. Guadalupe and Juanita went up to the bride-to-be and kissed her.

Juanita turned to Ermina, "How wonderful to see you, Ermina, on our side of the world. Welcome to Vegas."

"Las Vegas is so great, Juanita. And Jimmy the Pig and the staff have taken such good care of us – thank you. And, I've already made money at the slot machines!"

Juanita looked at Jimmy the Pig, who nodded, smiling.

"Well, this is just the beginning, Ermina – and tomorrow, of course, is the big day. And I'm going to need your help to wear my sari."

"Of course. And you must meet Pig Dog and Patty and Pearlie and Zack, who will be doing the ceremony.

"Ah, yes, the imperfect master," said Juanita. "But who are all these others?" looking around for Shri Vindaloo, who was playing a funny jumping game with Paloma and Delicia.

"Pig girls, come on," said Guadalupe, holding out her paws. "We should check in and freshen up. There's a lot to do all day today and tomorrow." Micaela joined the three of them in the elevator, and as the elevator doors closed, Guadalupe sent Shri Vindaloo a flying kiss. Shri Vindaloo caught it and pressed it to his heart.

Luiz and EunicePig were, of course, still, and forever, in each other's arms and eyes and hearts.

Leaving them in their joyful world, Shri Vindaloo took Juanita and Ermina, each by a paw, and, wandering into the bar, said, "Let's go meet the imperfect master."

They hadn't taken but a step through the doorway when Pearlie came bounding up and, in her usual manner, threw herself squealing on Shri Vindaloo. Zack, who was right behind her, said, "Greetings, can I interest you ladies, and you, of course, Shri Vindaloo, in a Vieux Carre – I've just discovered that the bartender is from New Orleans."

Juanita smiled at him, "I know, I recruited him."

The bartender brought around these wonderfully-elegant pink-tinted cocktails.

Ermina said, "It might be too strong for me."

"Just take a sip, Ermina," said Pearlie, "you'll taste the magic of New Orleans."

She did, and licked her lips, a new twinkle forming in her eye.

Shri Vindaloo took a swallow, "My god, the cocktails only get better, Zack. But, as we know, everything gets better every day."

Juanita smiled, "That's certainly true around you, Shri Vindaloo."

"It's such a pleasure to meet you, Juanita." Zack touched his lips to her bejeweled paw. "Shri Vindaloo told me you want a perfectly imperfect wedding for Luiz. And while I haven't met him yet, I feel I know him already – Shri Vindaloo told us about his magical courtship of EunicePig."

"So, Zack – or should I call you master or imperfect master…"

"You can call me anything you like, Juanita, but, like Shri Vindaloo, I like 'darling' the best."

"Well, how about 'imperfect darling'?"

"Even better – whaddya think Pearlie? Am I an imperfect darling?"

"You're perfectly imperfect, my darling."

Juanita, of course, persisted, "So, my imperfect darling, what will the ceremony be like?"

"Well, first I'd need to meet the bridal couple together. I've met EunicePig but I need to see her and Luiz together – their joy will trigger the feel of the ceremony. I like to keep things simple and, of course, keep bits of it secret. Shri Vindaloo, who is on both sides of the aisle, will explain the process to EunicePig and Luiz. And, as it unfolds, the rest of you just have to celebrate – may the God of your choice bless you."

The bartender brought over another round of Vieux Carres, just as Pig Dog and Patty waltzed in. they had clearly gone shopping and were all duded up and had a pink sequined cowboy hat for Ermina.

Pig Dog said, "I thought you needed a cowboy hat for the wedding, Ermina."

Patty put it on her head, she smiled shyly and everyone applauded.

Pig Dog kissed her cheek. "You look great, Ermina. But, be careful or be sure. You know the rule, right? If a lady pig puts her cowboy hat on a pig, it means she's going home with him that night."

Ermina blushed. "I'm too old for that."

"You're never too old for love, Ermina," Shri Vindaloo smiled. "Juanita, this is Patty and Pig Dog, friends of mine who live in the desert in California."

"Welcome – friends of Shri Vindaloo quickly become family," said Juanita. "And our family is from the desert region of Mexico, so I guess we're already relatives in a sense."

Patty smiled at her, "Well, neither of us is from the desert originally, but we moved there – separately – and we both love it."

"Welcome to the wedding. And it's so thoughful that you brought Ermina that shimmering cowboy hat. What are you going to wear to the wedding Ermina?"

"I was planning to wear a sari – I mean it is my daughter's wedding."

"Oh no, Ermina, let's go shopping and see what we can find that makes the cowboy hat really dance."

Ermina was deep into her second Vieux Carre, "OK, let's do it."

Zack said, "We're going to look for Luiz and EunicePig so we can get a feel for what the wedding will be like."

And as they all turned towards the entrance of the bar, there was Guadalupe, shimmering with the fragrance of love.

Shri Vindaloo jumped in the air and almost ran the few steps to her and folded her into him.

"Who is that amazing creature?" said Pearlie.

"That's my daughter, Guadalupe," said Juanita smiling happily, "and, it certainly looks like she is in love."

Shri Vindaloo brought her over and introduced her to the gang. "This is Guadalupe, Juanita's daughter, Luiz' sister, EunicePig's sister-in-law to be, and, well…" he looked overwhelmed, "we have to go now."

"Where are Paloma and Delicia? And Micaela?"

"Micaela is taking them on a helicopter ride to see the Hoover Dam so we can spend time together. He is still so thoughtful – I know now why I married him."

"He is – when he met me, he thanked me for loving you – what a gentle pig! And boy, does he look tasty?"

"Oh, yes," she smiled. They were holding each other in the elevator by then.

"The penthouse, my dear?" Shri Vindaloo asked her.

"Yes, pleaaase," said Guadalupe.

The young elevator operator smiled to himself. "Are you part of the wedding party?"

"Yes, yes, indeed," said Shri Vindaloo.

"Well, congratulations."

"Thank you," Shri Vindaloo crossed his palm with a large banknote, smiling. "But we are not the wedding couple."

"Well, you look very much in love."

"We are," said Guadalupe, as they alighted at the penthouse.

They entered his room and Shri Vindaloo was delighted to see that it was still early afternoon. He poured two glasses of champagne and matched the lipstick marks on the welcome note to her lips – a perfect fit, of course.

"Guadalupe," he sighed.

"Shri Vindaloo, I love you."

"I love you too, my darling."

And they slowly and deliciously melted into each other.

The sun was going down when they found the world again, and Guadalupe said, "The children must be back."

"Let's go find them."

"But they'll be tired and worn out. And Micaela will give them a bath and get them ready for bed."

"But let's go find them – I need to give them a few thousand kisses."

"That would be so much fun – except they won't be able to go to sleep, they'd be too excited."

"Well, that's OK – it is Tio Luiz' wedding, after all."

They dressed, helping each other, which, of course, took quite a bit of time. Guadalupe said, "I'll put them to bed – Micaela has to talk with Zack about tomorrow's program. But, I'll come back tonight, after they're asleep."

"But what about in the morning?"

"They can come and wake us."

And, sure enough, there was an eager thumping of small paws on the door early the next morning with excited squeals of "Mama, Shri Vindaloo, open the door."

Guadalupe ran to the door, slipping into a robe that was lying on a chair by the bed. "Good morning darlings." The little piggies bounded in jumping up and kissing her one at a time and together.

"Where's Shri Vindaloo?" asked Paloma.

"He's awake, but still in bed."

"Let's go wake him up properly." And both Paloma and Delicia ran excited into the bedroom and jumped on the bed. Shri Vindaloo sat up, the bedclothes slipping down his chest; Guadalupe slipped in beside him.

"Shri Vindaloo, we missed you," said Paloma, kissing him on the cheek. Delicia was on his other cheek. "We went up in a holocopter and I drove it in the air. Paloma did also."

They snuggled in between him and Guadalupe.

"Oh, that's amazing, did it fly really high up?"

"Really, really high – everything looked like ants."

"Except for the big dam that we went to see," said Paloma.

"But you're not wearing a shirt, Shri Vindaloo." Delicia was tickling Shri Vindaloo's chest.

"No," he said, laughing. "I don't usually sleep with a shirt."

"Of course," said Paloma, "that's because he's a boy pig."

"Papi was a boy pig," said Delicia, "but then he became a girl pig. Are you going to become a girl pig, Shri Vindaloo?"

"I hope not," said Guadalupe.

"No, no, definitely not," said Shri Vindaloo.

"Good," said Paloma. "Us too – we are girl pigs and we are NOT going to become boy pigs."

"Mama also," said Delicia.

"That's wonderful," said Shri Vindaloo.

"But, darlings, today is Tio Luiz' wedding, and we have to go get ready." Guadalupe climbed out of bed and pulled the little piggies off Shri Vindaloo so she had a chance to complete his proper good morning kiss.

"Oh, that's right," said Shri Vindaloo, stirring a bit under the sheets. "And have you met EunicePig – she's your new Tia?"

They both nodded enthusiastically. "She's so beautiful," said Delicia.

"She made us the same dresses as your shirt," said Paloma. "We love her."

"I do, too," said Shri Vindaloo.

Guadalupe leaned over for a proper see-you-later kiss and whisked the piggies out the door.

Shri Vindaloo yawned and stretched, delighting in the even richer fragrance of love that suffused the room.

The wedding was in a couple of hours and he had to meet with EunicePig and Luiz, separately, before that. He smiled and reached for the valet call button.

In an amazing thirty minutes (or so), Shri Vindaloo, coffee and croissanted and dressed in his wedding finery was at the elevator. He looked like an African monarch in a multi-colored printed silk robe, held together by a shimmering golden fabric belt across his girth. On his head, he had a crown with occasionally flashing lights. Guadalupe had brought these for him from Mexico, obviously aware that the dictum – thou shalt not upstage the bride – did not apply to Shri Vindaloo.

By the time he got to the lobby, he immediately saw a harried Luiz, looking for him high and low.

"Shri Vindaloo, thank God you're here."

"Ah, the bridegroom-to-be! How handsome you look. A great day for you – for all of us."

"But, Shri Vindaloo," he spoke softly, urgently, pulling Shri Vindaloo into a quiet corner. "I haven't yet told EunicePig... y'know, about..." He glanced furtively towards his private area.

Shri Vindaloo was perplexed for a moment – then suddenly it dawned. "Oh, Luiz, don't worry about that. Don't worry about a thing. EunicePig is a modern girl and – most important – she loves you. And in any case, as Guadalupe says, it's a blessing not a curse."

Luiz clung to Shri Vindaloo's paw. "Do you really think so?"

"Of course, my friend. I think we both need a glass of champagne," waving out to Jimmy the Pig, who was talking to Zack and Pearlie.

"And where is EunicePig?"

"I don't know," said a recovering Luiz. "I haven't seen her since yesterday evening when she and Ermina went up to their suite."

Pearlie, who was in a svelte (by her standards) green sheath and her green boa, came jumping up as usual, but stopped short of throwing herself on him, amazed and overwhelmed by his regalia. "Shri Vindaloo, you look so... so regal – I don't know whether to kiss you or bow at your feet."

"Darling," he spread his paws wide, pursing his snout. "Come and get it."

And, of course, she did. But she quickly pulled back, "And what about Guadalupe? I've never seen you so... so taken, and you are generally quite easily taken. Why haven't you told us about her yet?"

"Well, Pearlie, it all happened so fast. I had met her in Mexico City right before I met you and Zack. She was amazing, but she was married, so, y'know, I had to hold the love in."

"Shri Vindaloo, you are a pig in a million."

"And then she came to Goa, with Luiz and Juanita and... everything happened. Her husband, Miguel, was in the middle of a sex reassignment – have you met Micaela, yet? She is also amazing – and we, Guadalupe and I fell in love on the banks of the Mandovi."

"Shri Vindaloo, that is just so lovely," she still held him close. "But I can still swoop down and kiss you, right?"

"Darling, you have no choice and neither do I."

The elevator doors opened and Paloma and Delicia, in the prettiest turquoise taffeta dresses, ran into the lobby and up to Shri Vindaloo. Guadalupe and Micaela followed them smiling.

Pearlie pulled Guadalupe aside and kissed her, more gently that anyone thought possible. "Guadalupe, thank you. I love you. Now that I know, you are even more beautiful than when I saw you earlier."

Guadalupe smiled happiness and, leaning over, kissed Pearlie back. She was wearing a turquoise lame dress, which looked like Mexico City, with, of course, navy and turquoise stilettos. She had a blue feather boa about her neck, and Pearlie smiled knowingly.

Micaela was in a flaming red sheath, showing off her voluptuous bosom and with miles and miles of thigh showing on both sides. She blew Pearlie a winking kiss.

Pearlie blinked, thinking, if this wasn't Vegas, she would be arrested.

Zack came up to them, a little distracted. "We've got to leave for the chapel. Patty and Pig Dog are already there and we still have to get a few things organized – a few surprises." He was dressed in a white linen suit with his face all pale as if it had white make-up. He looked like he had seen a vision – Shri Vindaloo had never seen him like this.

The Imperfect Master was in the house.

He pulled Pearlie away from the show and they took off for the venue.

The elevator doors opened again and everyone turned to look.

Juanita stepped out, a pink maharani in her chiffon sari and a monster pink sapphire ring with a matching set of earrings and necklace.

Shri Vindaloo was rocked back, and as he was recovering, Ermina followed her out. This really sent him reeling – she had on a pink spangly jumpsuit, her pink cowboy hat and pink heels, matching the pair Juanita had on. And she was wearing Juanita's pink boa in a devil-may-care throw across her shoulders. WOW! This had to be the most glamorous mothers of the bridal couple anywhere.

There was a rising crescendo of wows, look at them's all through the lobby. Jimmy the Pig had the photographers going wild.

And then, the bride stepped out. Time simply stopped.

She wore a simple white bridal dress with a modest train, but the joy on her face showed why no one could ever upstage a bride on her wedding day. She ran up and hugged Shri Vindaloo and everyone in the lobby clapped spontaneously.

"Shri Vindaloo," she whispered. "I don't know what to say. I love you, of course, but…"

"Darling, darling, darling, darling…" He was at loss for words. With Guadalupe nearby and EunicePig, in her bridal finery, in his arms, love and joy were everywhere. He smiled even more foolishly than usual.

'Shri Vindaloo, you know we are leaving for Paris right after the wedding. But, I have carefully trained Sarita to take care of you till I get back. Will you be alright?"

"Darling, darling, darling, darling…"

"Tia EunicePig, Tia EunicePig," the little piggies chorused, and taking her by her paws, pulled her to Luiz, who was sitting on a sofa in what looked like a trance.

"My beautiful, lovely, wonderful darling," he whispered.

"My beautiful, lovely, wonderful soon-to-be-husband," kissing him modestly.

Jimmy the Pig escorted them – contrary to common custom, EunicePig and Luiz were to ride together to the wedding – to a limousine that was a familiar shade of yellow. Juanita smiled happily, as she and Ermina and Shri Vindaloo got into a pink limousine. Guadalupe, Micaela and the jumping piglets climbed, of course, into a blue one. And they all left for the wedding.

The wedding venue was a converted Elvis chapel. Pig Dog had set up a bar along the side, and leaning over the bar was a hot young thing dressed in a sequined figure-hugging dress with, of course, feathers out the back. She turned around as the wedding party entered, and Shri Vindaloo was amazed – and delighted – that it was Patty. He had known her as the smart, intellectual writer, the slightly less-than elegant western woman the colour of the desert, and now this.

She called out, "Hey, Shri Vindaloo, tell me about Guadalupe." He went over and kissed her. Pig Dog salaamed him, "Well done, pardner."

By this time, Guadalupe had arrived and, with the pretty piglets in tow, came across to them. Micaela had disappeared.

Shri Vindaloo had his paws open. "What's to tell, Patty, Pig Dog – this is Guadalupe, and this is Paloma, and this is Delicia, and this is my life."

"And what a life!" said Patty, delighted. "And look at the mothers-in-law to be! And, ohmyGod – the wedding couple!"

EunicePig and Luiz had walked in to a joyous smattering of applause. They nodded, smiling, to everyone, and went off to the small podium at the front of the chapel.

Pig Dog opened bottles of champagne and Patty passed the coupes around. "A toast, a toast," said Pig Dog, "to the two most beautiful mothers-in-law in the world."

Juanita and Ermina went up to the bar, happy. Ermina tugged her cowboy hat tightly on her head. "I'm holding on to this," she said.

They all laughed. Paloma and Delicia had got loose and were running around. "Where's Papi?" Delicia asked.

He peeped his head from behind a curtain at the back of the podium. "I'm here, angelitos," he called out. "You sit with Mama and Mama Lagarto."

Shri Vindaloo went up to the podium. "We're all here – and, now.... here's the Imperfect Master!"

Everyone applauded as Zack came out from behind the curtain. Shri Vindaloo took a seat in the front row.

"Dearly beloved – and all that jazz. We here today to celebrate Eunice Pig [cheers around the room] and Luiz [more cheers, some in Spanish]. The couple bounced up to the podium, smiling nervously.

He took each of their paws and held them up in the air. He kissed each of them in turn, and then slowly brought their paws together. Looking around, he called out, "Shri Vindaloo!"

"Oh, yes." Shri Vindaloo jumped up from his seat and hurried to the podium and, from within his flowing garb, took out two matched jewelry boxes. He gave on to Luiz, who opened it to most delicate, almost embroidered ring, sparkling with tiny ojos de lagarto, which he slipped onto EunicePig's finger and kissed her lips, for the first time ever. EunicePig gasped, then recovering, opened the other jewelry box and put Luiz' ring on his finger – it was a simple gold band with a heart and her name engraved inside.

"I now pronounce you in love forever, EunicePig and Luiz, and married under the laws of the god of your choice."

Juanita had a deep happy smile, Ermina wiped tears from her eyes, and Pearlie burst into loud happy sobs.

"And now," announced Zack, "I give you Micaela!"

Pig Dog turned on the music and, of course, Elvis blasted from the speakers – VIVA LAS VEGAS! Micaela mouthed the words and almost danced out of her sheath. Paloma and Delicia bounced along in their seats, clapping in time, while all the male pigs had their eyes popping out – her floor show was definitely going to be a big draw.

"And now," said Micaela, "a song from Luiz to EunicePig." He signaled to Pig Dog and as the first strains of Love me Tender began, she sang more tenderly than you would have thought possible from the last dance.

Luiz and EunicePig, in a forever embrace, were in tears. "Thank you, Micaela," Luiz stammered out.

Guadalupe and Juanita, of course, knew Micaela's skills, but all the others were amazed at her extraordinary range. They all applauded loudly, except Delicia and Paloma. "That's too slow, Papi," Paloma called out. "We want a fast song."

"OK," she said, with a smile. "So, here's one from EunicePig for Luiz."

It was a moonlit night in old Mexico
I walked alone between some old adobe haciendas.

Delicia and Paloma were excited.

Suddenly, I heard the plaintive cry of a young Mexican girl

The piggies were out of their seats jumping up and down

You better come home, Speedy Gonzalez
Away from tannery row...

Everybody was out of their seats dancing sillily to the silly song; Pig Dog had made up a few pitchers of margaritas and, of course, there was a line-up of shots on the bar.

The party began.

And went on for a few hours till it was time for EunicePig and Luiz to leave for the airport for their honeymoon. They all burst out of the chapel and EunicePig, running to the limousine, threw her bocquet over her shoulder and it landed squarely between Patty and Pearlie.

Shri Vindaloo called out, "More weddings in the family," as the celebrations packed up.

Pig Dog and Patty had to drive back to the desert. They had asked Ermina to come stay with them, to show off her cowboy hat if nothing else. She was certainly tempted – Pig Dog had taken such good care of her – but she had decided to go to Mexico with Juanita.

Zack had somehow changed from his prelate avatar and was back to the man about town and Pearlie. "The Vieux Carre is waiting for you, my friend," said Zack, as Pearlie delivered yet one more of her tastiest smackeroos to Shri Vindaloo. They had to get to the airport for their flight to New Orleans.

Rounds of kisses and happiness and a few more cocktails later, the thinned-out wedding party – Shri Vindaloo, Ermina, Juanita, Guadalupe, Micaela and the little piggies – headed back to the hotel. The Lagarto plane was to leave for Mexico City in a couple of hours so Shri Vindaloo and Guadalupe rode in one limo and the others in the other.

When they arrived at the hotel, Paloma came running up to Guadalupe, "Mama, why don't you and Shri Vindaloo say hasta la vista properly upstairs?"

Out of the mouth of babes, thought Shri Vindaloo, as he escorted Guadalupe up to the suite.

They were late coming down, of course, but it was a private plane so it could wait. And after many more rounds of kisses and Spanish and other endearments, the Lagartos left for the airport.

Shri Vindaloo went into the bar and ordered an Old Fashioned. He smiled. What a fantastic wedding; what a blessed life, he thought. He sipped his drink, and a joyous flavour tinged his smile.

He ordered another drink and, as it was served, he noticed a very beautiful pig at the end of the bar. She looked very familiar, but he had to look away from her – it was impossible to not look at her very lovely bosom, which appeared to be pouring out the top of her dress. He looked away.

He thought about Guadalupe and Paloma and Delicia, and Guadalupe again. He was so blessed.

"Shri Vindaloo!" the girl pig at the bar called out.

He had to turn back. He smiled at her – she did look familiar. And he couldn't believe her breasts didn't just roll out onto the bar.

"Don't you remember me? I am Tatiana from the circus. We flew through the air together."

"Tatiana, of course. I remember you – how you held me! Thank you so much. What a delight to see you again."

He took his drink across to where she was sitting. He smiled into her eyes, not daring to look down. "That was an amazing adventure – you are so strong. And so beautiful. And I see you have such long fingernails – but I didn't feel them when you held me so close."

She finished her drink and smiled invitingly.

"How do you do a trapeze act with such long fingernails? Isn't it dangerous?"

"If you come upstairs, Shri Vindaloo, I can show you."

He glanced down at her chest. A Frank Sinatra song was playing on the jukebox.

It's the wrong time
And the wrong place
Though your lips are lovely
They're the wrong lips

She leaned further forward.

They're not her lips
But they're such lovely lips…

He reached over and kissed her sweetly on the cheek.

"Thank you darling. But I can't fly through the air with you again."

He signalled the bartender to put the drinks on his tab, and, with a wistful smile, went up to his suite.